RETURN TO BARRADALE

Melody has sworn never to return to Barradale, the island where she'd grown up — and been so unhappy . . . Now, living in Glasgow, she has forged a new life in the City for herself. But when the gorgeous Kieran Matthews turns up on her doorstep, demanding that she should go back with him to see her sick sister, she finds she cannot refuse. And for Melody, family secrets must be unravelled before Kieran's love can help to resolve her past.

Books by Carol MacLean
in the Linford Romance Library:

WILD FOR LOVE
RESCUE MY HEART

CAROL MacLEAN

RETURN TO BARRADALE

Complete and Unabridged

LINFORD
Leicester

First published in Great Britain in 2012

First Linford Edition
published 2013

A catalogue record for this book is available
from the British Library.

ISBN 978–1–4448–1540–5

Published by
F. A. Thorpe (Publishing)
Anstey, Leicestershire

Set by Words & Graphics Ltd.
Anstey, Leicestershire
Printed and bound in Great Britain by
T. J. International Ltd., Padstow, Cornwall

This book is printed on acid-free paper

1

The man standing on Melody's doorstep was tall and broad-shouldered with the darkest blue eyes she had ever seen. Those eyes looked at her with cool disdain as he said brusquely, 'I've come to fetch you home.'

Melody took an involuntary step back into her house. He seemed to take this as an invitation into her home, brushing past her to stand with hands shoved deep into the pockets of his jeans and the toe of his boot tapping impatiently on the parquet floor.

Nice boots, she noticed. Good leather, well-heeled and hand-stitched. Not designer boots, but certainly made to last. And casting another glance at her unwelcome guest, Melody imagined they would need to be. He had a rugged outdoor look to him and his jacket couldn't hide outlines of well-muscled arms. He was clearly someone who undertook physical work on a regular basis.

'Melody Harper,' she introduced herself, holding her hand out confidently and speaking with just an edge of unconcealed sarcasm. 'And you are?'

He stared at her hand for a moment but made no move to shake it, so she let it drop. He frowned, brows closing together — black, like his thick shock of hair.

'I know who you are,' he said and she caught a lilt of Irish in his voice, dark and velvet. 'I'm Kieran Matthews. I'm here on your sister's behalf. She wants to see you.'

'Skye?' Which was a stupid thing to say. She only had one sister, four years younger than her. 'Why? Is she all right?'

'No, she's not,' he told her bluntly. He started walking around the room as if to let out pent-up energy, picking up ornaments and placing them down again. Melody waited for him to tell her more, sensing he needed time to find the words.

The main room of the ground floor was huge, with wooden flooring and bright with light from full height windows. She saw him frown again in puzzlement as he saw the mannequin in the middle of the room, draped in its wedding gown. It was a beautiful creation, all delicate ivory silk with pearl buttons and frothy tulle under the skirts. It wasn't quite finished, but she still had a fortnight to do so before the wedding.

'You're getting married?'

'Listen, just tell me what's happened to Skye.' It was her turn to be blunt. It wasn't really his business, was it, whether she was getting married or not? She was caught between a sudden annoyance at his hostile attitude and a fear for Skye.

Kieran sank down onto the sofa under the window and ran a hand through his hair, leaving it even more tousled.

'She's not well. I don't mean physically,' he said quickly when Melody gave a little gasp of shock. 'She's down in the dumps. But not the sort we all get from time to time when things aren't going

3

well. With her it just won't lift. Lately she's been asking for you.'

'For me? Why?'

'I honestly don't know. I had got the distinctly strong impression that the two of you weren't close.'

'It's not uncommon in families, you know,' Melody retorted. 'Especially as there's a big age gap between us. We never liked the same things or wanted to do stuff together.'

She knew she was being defensive. She didn't have to explain herself to this large, unwelcome stranger!

But there was guilt — there always had been — that she and her only sister didn't get along better. Whenever she thought about Skye — which was, quite deliberately, not often — Melody found herself wondering whether she should have tried harder to get to know her.

'Well, whatever the deal is between you, she wants to see you now. The fact of the matter is that she's never got over Fiona's death.'

'But that was over a year ago. Surely

she's come to terms with it by now? I know it was devastating and awful, but are you seriously telling me Skye's been depressed all year?'

Skye's best friend Fiona had been killed in a freak climbing accident in the Cairngorm Mountains.

'Well if you ever visited your estranged family, you'd know, wouldn't you?' Kieran returned icily.

Estranged family. She'd never thought of it like that. She wasn't estranged from them, was she? Okay, she was extremely busy with her career in Glasgow's Merchant City, but she phoned her mother occasionally to keep in touch. And they visited . . .

With a jolt Melody realised it was over a year since she'd seen them, when she had returned to Barradale for Fiona's funeral. She had literally flown to the island's tiny airport, gone to the service and wake afterwards, and flown home to Glasgow the same evening.

She simply couldn't afford more time away, she had told herself. Her first collection was on display at Sara's boutique in the East End and she had to be there. As it was, one of the models had tripped on the catwalk and ripped a hem. She shuddered to think what would have happened if she hadn't been there to mend the damage fast and accurately.

'That's not fair,' she protested. 'If things with Skye are so bad why has my mother not mentioned it to me?'

'Maeve won't want to worry or upset you. She thinks the world of you, you know.'

The stony look on his face implied that he didn't share her mother's admiration. Well, who was he to judge her!

'Who are you, exactly?' she asked annoyed. 'I don't remember meeting you last year.'

'I'm a friend of your parents and a friend of Skye's. I was away on business in Europe last year when Fiona had her terrible accident and I couldn't get home in time for the funeral. I arrived a day later, in fact, but of course you were already gone by then.

'I went back to live in Barradale four years ago and became friendly with Maeve and John. They talk a lot about you — Melody's done this, Melody's done that, Melody's won an award. I was quite surprised that you never came to visit in all that time.'

He didn't know the history behind it. He couldn't know how much it had cost her to return to Barradale, however briefly, for the funeral. She had sworn never to go back once she'd made a life for herself on the mainland.

The doorbell rang loudly in the still, tense air between them. She left him sitting there and opened the door to see Leila Doves aglow with an expression of hopeful anticipation.

'Is it ready? Oh, do say it's finished.' She clasped her hands together and squealed in delight when she saw the mannequin. 'Oh, it's gorgeous! Clever you. Can I try it on?'

'It's not quite ready. You need at least two more fittings. I'm not happy with the bodice and the skirt is still too long.'

Leila clutched at her chest in dramatic fright. 'It'll be ready for the wedding, won't it? What'll I tell Sam if we have to delay again? He'll kill me!'

Leila and Sam's wedding plans were an epic tale of stormy arguments and lavish reunions. The last disagreement had seen Leila throw off her engagement ring, which had promptly vanished into the sand of the beach they were picnicking on, never to be found again. The wedding was delayed while the couple made their peace and Sam saved up for a replacement ring. In the meantime Leila had decided she hated her crimson off-the-rack wedding dress and wanted a pure, classic look, made to measure from a designer.

This was where Melody had entered the picture. Although she had grown fond of Leila over the weeks of ideas, sketches, material samples and endless measuring and fitting, she admitted to herself she'd be glad when Leila and Sam finally tied the knot and disappeared together over the horizon.

'Oh, sorry, I didn't realise you had company,' Leila said, noticing Kieran for the first time.

He stood up politely.

'He was just leaving,' Melody said firmly, fixing him with a steely stare.

'Actually,' he said slowly, 'I think I'll stay. I'm going to drive you back to Barradale but there's plenty of time before we have to leave.'

'You're leaving? Now?' Leila's voice rose.

Melody shook her head as if she could dislodge Leila by doing so. She looked at Kieran.

He was a solid man and at least six foot two tall. If he didn't want to budge, then she couldn't make him. She wished he would turn his unsettling dark blue eyes somewhere else, away from her. He was too attractive for his own good, she thought, and probably used to getting his own way because of it. Well, he had another think coming if he imagined he could ride roughshod over her. She would let him stay until

Leila Doves had gone, then she would get rid of him.

'Okay, you can use the back living room,' she told him. She showed him through into a pleasant spacious room at the back of the house. 'The kitchen's through there. Please help yourself to tea or coffee. I won't be long.'

★ ★ ★

Leila's eyes glistened with tears. 'Sorry,' she sniffled, 'I suddenly imagined you going away and leaving my lovely dress half done and then me having to get married in a horrible dress from a shop.'

Melody bit down on her lip, took a deep breath and soothed her client. 'It'll be fine, Leila, trust me. Now just try this on so I can adjust the line of the buttons.'

'When are you coming back?' Leila persisted, turning with her arms up so Melody could tuck and pin.

'If I do go, then I won't be away

more than a few days. There's ample time to finish the dress.'

'That reminds me.' Leila grabbed her voluminous woven handbag, springing pins as she did so, and produced a thick, glossy magazine. 'I couldn't believe it when I saw my dress in here. I'm so excited that I'll be wearing a wedding dress featured in Wedding Today magazine. You must be thrilled.'

'Can I see that?' Melody asked sharply.

'Of course. Is anything the matter? I thought you'd be glad of the publicity. The dress looks marvellous. It's not the real thing, simply divine artistic sketches, but it's clearly my dress.'

Melody stared intently at the article and sketches, with Leila peering over her shoulder still gushing about the design.

'Oh, that's funny.' Leila paused in confusion. 'I hadn't noticed before, it's not your name on it after all. It's part of the Catherine Sommerlee Collection . . . how odd . . . how did that happen, do you think?'

Melody closed the magazine slowly

and gave it back to Leila who was looking distressed. She had the previous month's issue of the magazine lying on top of her bedside cabinet where she had placed it, wanting to think about its content before acting. Now she could add this one. She realised that she needed to speak to Harry — and soon.

'It's coincidence, that's all,' Melody said lightly. 'In fact if you look closely there are several differences in details and finish. It's a different dress, after all.'

Leila was easily reassured and was happy to stand patiently until Melody was satisfied. She went away with the promise that Melody would call her immediately upon her return to Glasgow and that, no, she really wouldn't be away for very long at all.

* * *

Melody went through to check on Kieran. He was comfortably at home and relaxed, with his long legs stretched out in front of him, sipping a cup of coffee and flicking through a fashion magazine with an air of indifference. Not his thing, obviously. As if she cared.

'You're not getting married,' he said. Did she detect a note of relief in his voice? Possibly because it would spoil his plans. She could hardly rush off to Barradale island with him if she was planning to get married soon.

'No,' she agreed.

'I'll wait while you pack.'

'I can't just up and leave now! I'm trying to run a business here. I have clients and deadlines.'

'Are they more important than your own sister?'

'No, of course not. But does Skye really want me to come to her? Maybe a change of scene would do her good. She could come and stay with me.'

She realised that she was talking too fast, throwing out suggestions, anything to stave off going back to Barradale.

'You really are selfish, aren't you?'

His tone was cold disgust as if she had just confirmed what he knew all along.

No! she wanted to cry. *You don't understand. I have the unreasoning fear that if I ever returned to Barradale I'd never escape. I'd be swallowed up just as before; a nonentity, unfulfilled and voiceless.*

Instead she said boldly, 'It goes with the territory. I work in a cut-throat industry where it's a positive bonus.' Let him think what he liked. What did she care?

'I'm not leaving without you,' he stated. 'So you may as well get ready.'

Melody sighed. 'Very well. I'll come for a few days and see Skye. If she's really as depressed as you say, then I'll bring her back with me to Glasgow and get her some help. I really can't leave my business for long. If you're a businessman you'll understand that. That's the deal. Take it or leave it.'

He nodded. 'Fair enough.'

Melody filled her suitcase with all the items she might need, her hands

14

trembling. This was the worst possible time to be leaving. The article about Catherine Sommerlee ran through her mind, along with the other magazine's contents. She had to speak to Harry.

Harry! What would he think when he discovered she'd gone to Barradale without telling him? And there was Sara, and Niall, and the others. She dreaded to think what they would say. Their planned, large fashion show was only a few weeks away and they were already behind schedule.

On the other hand, if Skye needed her as desperately as Kieran Matthews claimed, then she had to go to her. She didn't know her sister very well but she was family, and the ties that bind never unfasten entirely.

It was strange that her mother hadn't mentioned any concerns for her younger daughter during phone calls, she fretted. Perhaps it was all a false alarm, and she would be able to return home quickly.

She dragged her smart little suitcase on its tiny wheels out of her bedroom and slowly clunked it down the stairs where Kieran was waiting in the hall. She pulled on her coat, belted it tightly and then paused to check her make-up in the mirror.

'You're not wearing those, are you?'

She looked down at her feet in surprise, following his gaze. She was wearing her favourite Blahnik green sandals with their incredibly slender high heels.

'What's wrong with them?'

He shrugged. 'There are no city streets up there, if you remember. And have you got a thicker coat? That little thing won't keep out the island wind.'

Melody cast a mental list of what she had packed — cotton shirts, woollen dress trousers, a lovely satin dress, a gilet, gauzy underthings and silk pyjamas, plus four pairs of her shoes. Enough, surely, for a short trip.

Kieran took her fleece-lined leather pilot's coat from its hook and gave it to her. He lifted her suitcase easily and led the way to his black land ranger.

'We should make the four o'clock

ferry without too much of a rush,' he said over his shoulder.

Without a word Melody got into the vehicle and strapped herself in. With a mounting sense of dread, she realised she was indeed about to return to Barradale.

2

Kieran was angry with himself. He hadn't handled the situation well. He'd let his emotions rule him and that, as he well knew, was always a mistake.

He looked across at the woman leaning against the railing of the ferry. The stiff wind was lifting her thick rope of auburn hair and blowing wayward curls around her face and into her eyes, but she didn't appear to notice. Her face was white and immobile as she watched the island loom closer out of the damp mist. A few lights twinkled along Barradale's coast, breaking through the early evening's dull veil.

He had been prepared to meet a shallow, vain and selfish woman, which was how he had pictured Melody from all the things he had heard about her.

It wasn't that her family described her that way. They had reasons — excuses,

Kieran privately thought — for her life-style and her neglect of them, but it was clear to Kieran that she pleased herself above others. Why else did she never visit her parents and sister? He still felt that she was all those things he had named her, but what he hadn't reckoned on was the physical impact she'd had on him.

She was beautiful. Her glossy hair framed a face with high cheekbones, flawless skin and large hazel eyes, dark-fringed. She was tall for a woman, easily five-ten — or more in her ridiculous heels — and her shape was voluptuously curved, like that of a painting of an early-era goddess.

He was absolutely and completely drawn to her, which made him angry with his own chemistry as he had no intention of being attracted to such a woman.

And yet his initial reaction to seeing the wedding dress had been a sharp disappointment that she was . . . what? Unavailable? It was ludicrous of him, as was the shaft of relief when he realised the dress was for someone else. Her mother hadn't said that she designed wedding dresses, only that she designed and made clothes. Probably she didn't know, either.

Kieran turned towards the blast of wind funnelled by the ferry bow and let its rawness slap some sense into him. All he had to do was deliver Melody Harper home to her sister, Skye. End of story.

Still her words rang in his ears. He had accused her of being selfish and she hadn't even tried to deny it. *It goes with the territory. I work in a cut-throat industry where it's a positive bonus,* she'd said. She was proud of it. He'd practically had to drag her into the car for the journey to Barradale to see her own flesh and blood.

The ferry's horn blasted, long and timbrous, heralding their arrival at Barradale harbour. Kieran breathed in a heady mixture of fresh air, salt rime and seaweed as the crew shouted and threw great tarry ropes to secure them to the iron bollards on the pier. He was home, back in the haven of Barradale.

Automatically he scanned the waiting crowd on the quayside for Elspeth, but she wasn't there. Never mind; he'd catch up with her at the house once he had escorted his reluctant companion to her parents' home.

With any luck he wouldn't have to cross paths with Ms Melody Harper during her stay on the island at all. In fact, he'd make sure of it. There was still a steady stream of tourists visiting the island and he would be busy catering to their needs. When she'd gone, he would soon forget that unexpected and unwanted animal magnetism. It would fade like a passing fancy.

★ ★ ★

Melody had tried phoning Harry twice during the crossing, but reception was patchy and the connection had cut off before she could speak to him. She shivered in spite of her leather coat. It was a raw wind, with unseasonable hints of winter, and she felt her spirits dip like the low-troughed waves into which the ferry slipped as it went further and further from the mainland towards Barradale's dark shore.

She'd been surprised and grateful when Kieran brought her a paper cup of hot coffee from the ferry's diner, but apart from that he hadn't spoken to her, preferring to stand mid-deck watching the sea. It was fine by her. She was alone in the crowd once again. It reminded her of the previous week at Harry's birthday party . . .

* * *

Harry had turned thirty, although he dressed and acted more like twenty. He'd sent round an invitation to a private function at a well-known Glasgow night club.

'You of course will be my number

one guest, sweetie,' he said flirtatiously when he met Melody for a quick coffee at lunch time in a coffee shop in Merchant City.

'Along with all your other 'number one' guests.' Melody laughed good-naturedly.

Harry flicked an assessing eye over a young woman entering the coffee shop. She smiled back at him. He had that effect on women with his boyishly eager features, designer stubble beard and careless blond hair.

'You're so cruel, Melody dearest,' he said in mock-hurt, his eyes still on the girl. 'Why don't you let me take you to dinner so you can make amends to me?'

'I don't think so,' Melody said. 'Unless it's just a friend asking a friend.'

'More like a hot date,' he said hopefully, turning back to her.

'You never give up, do you Harry?' she said with some exasperation. 'It's in the past now; we were young college students and we lasted — how long?

— a couple of months of going out before we split up.'

'It was a great couple of months, though, and I'm older and more mature now — hey, I'm turning thirty, for goodness' sake! Let's try again.'

'Drop it,' she warned him. 'Anyway, can you take a look at these designs I've sketched? I'd love your opinion on them.'

She sipped her coffee thoughtfully while Harry bent his blond head to scrutinise her drawings.

Harry, Melody, her best friend Sara, and Sara's boyfriend, Niall had all gone to art school at the same time. When they graduated they had decided to form an artistic support group for each other to help them all get started in what was a tough industry to become successful in. Harry had taken his love of photography and started photographing fashion shoots, shows and anything in that line. He had started writing freelance articles too, and hoped eventually to have his own magazine.

Melody was determined to form her own clothes label, while Sara and Niall had decided to open a clothes shop selling vintage, designer and unusual one-off items.

'Are Sara and Niall coming to the party?' she asked Harry.

'I certainly hope so. They owe me big time for that article I did on their east end 'surprise find' boutique.'

'What do you think of my ideas?'

'They're great, sweetie. I'd be happy to photograph the finished dresses.' He paused to hand them back to her and waited until she had zipped them into her portfolio case. 'You don't happen to know if Cath's back from Paris?'

'Cath?' Melody raised one eyebrow. 'Do you mean Catherine Sommerlee? I didn't know you two were pals.' She was surprised and more than a little horrified.

Catherine Sommerlee was a bridal designer who was starting to make a name for herself in Glasgow. Melody had met her at a few functions and workshops but, in spite of trying to chat to her, had found her to be aloof and unfriendly.

Harry flushed. 'I don't know her that well. I just thought I'd invite her to the party. It'll be a fun evening but also a chance to network. We're never off the leash, darling, you know that.'

'That's true. I'd better dash now, I've got a client coming at two for a fitting. See you at the party.' She gave him a quick kiss on the cheek and left him there, already grinning disarmingly at the pretty Oriental waitress.

* * *

The party was in full swing by the time Melody arrived, clutching the mandatory bottle of champagne and a beautifully wrapped present for Harry.

'Over here,' came the shouts and she saw Sara and Niall waving from a table at the corner of the dance floor. She pushed through gyrating bodies and a humid wall of perfume across the dance floor to find them. They were tucked behind an edge of wall which masked the music somewhat, allowing them to chat without having to shout.

'Where's the birthday boy, then?' Melody asked as she sat down to join them.

'Embarrassing himself on the dance floor.' Sara pointed behind them, giggling.

Melody looked over and after a few seconds located Harry dancing in his own peculiar style to an Eighties remix.

'Who's the gorgeous blonde dancing with him?' Niall asked, his tongue practically hanging out. Sara nudged him sharply. 'Ouch. I'm only asking.'

'That's Catherine Sommerlee,' Melody said in astonishment. 'And unlike Harry, she can actually dance.'

She watched the tall, willowy girl move gracefully to the beat, her platinum hair luminescing under the UV lighting, giving her an almost alien glow. Harry danced round her rather too closely, Melody thought, but Catherine was more than capable of keeping him at a suitable distance by subtly dancing away and back again as required.

'Is that the real Catherine Sommerlee? Gosh! I hope Harry brings her over and introduces us,' Sara said eagerly. 'It would be fantastic to get some of her clothes into our boutique.'

As if on cue Harry wove his way towards them, Catherine following languidly. Harry's face had a sheen of perspiration and he was clearly enjoying his own party.

'Darlings.' He raised a glass of champagne unsteadily, managing to spill a quantity onto the table. 'To me, Harry Gordon, no longer in his twenties, boohoo!'

'Don't be silly, you're still young and handsome,' Sara laughed, pulling him down into a seat at the table.

'Aren't you going to introduce us, Harry?' Niall asked, gesturing to Catherine to join them and gallantly pulling up a chair from another table across for her.

Sara gave him a warning glare as Harry waved expansively at the group.

'Catherine, these are my lovely friends. Friends, this is the lovely Catherine.'

Catherine Sommerlee slid gracefully into the proffered chair. She was like a beautiful white swan, Melody decided. She was blessed with extraordinarily glossy hair, so blonde it was almost white, a long slender neck and slim figure. She made Melody feel large and clumsy in comparison.

'Harry told us you design wedding dresses,' Sara gushed. 'Niall and I have our own boutique and we'd just love it if we could showcase your clothes.'

Catherine just looked at her. Her eyes were unusually dark for such pale skin and hair. Sara wriggled uncomfortably and Niall made a show of pouring more sparkling wine into glasses.

Melody felt she'd be sick if she drank any more, it was so hot and clammy in the room with its coloured glittering lights and the endless boom of the music. She lifted her hair off the nape of her neck to cool it and felt Catherine's gaze like a cold draught, assessing her.

'You're Melody? Harry was telling me that you design wedding dresses, too?' There was a European inflexion in her speech even though Melody was pretty sure Harry had said Catherine came from Oxford like himself. It made her sound mysterious, which was probably why she did it.

'That's right,' Melody replied easily. 'I'm the competition.'

It was meant to be a light joke to break the ice socially, but Catherine's eyes flashed.

'I always win, whatever I do,' she said dangerously.

Sara and Niall glanced at Melody in embarrassed silence. Unsure what to say, she was glad of the interruption when a young girl hurried up to them.

'Sorry I'm late, Catherine.' She looked around at everyone. 'Hi, I'm Jade, Catherine's assistant.' She sat down heavily next to Melody and began biting her nails anxiously — they were already bitten to the quick.

'Do stop that,' Catherine commented

irritably. 'Really, Jade, you knew this was a party — why didn't you change before you came?'

The girl looked down at herself with a confused expression. She was wearing maroon velvet trousers and a cream silk shirt which unfortunately showed up every ounce of excess weight and did nothing for her freckled complexion and red hair.

'Straight off the boat from the islands — what can you do?' Catherine commented to no one in particular, but inviting them all to share her cruel humour.

Sara and Niall laughed obligingly but Melody was aghast. Did they need Catherine's patronage so badly for the shop that they would abandon common kindness and courtesy?

Then Harry lumbered into the conversation, raising his filled glass yet again and slurring the words.

'Melody's an island girl too, aren't you, darling?'

It was never clear to Melody then or

afterwards whether Harry was simply drunk and contributing vaguely to the conversation or whether he meant to deliberately land her in it.

'Oh dear. It must be difficult for you, losing the accent and finding social poise,' Catherine said poisonously.

'Remember, you did have that accent,' Sara chipped in. 'You had to smooth it out.'

Suddenly it was as if the table had a line drawn down it. On one side sat Melody and Jade, the outsiders. On the other side sat Catherine, playing queen bee to her willing sycophants. Niall and Harry were besotted with her looks and even Sara, who was supposed to be Melody's best friend, was across the other side of the table with unfriendly eyes, hoping for Catherine's approval with her barbed comment about Melody's accent.

Everything shifted. Melody had built up a new life for herself with what she believed were supportive good friends who would back her in any situation.

Now she knew the painful reality of being utterly alone in a throng of people, even if only for a few seconds.

It was gone so quickly that she was able to reassure herself that she had imagined it, but she couldn't forget the sensation of being isolated, friendless. It played over in her mind every so often in the days to come.

While she sat there the talk moved on, then someone had fallen over on the dance floor and everyone was laughing at the spectacle. Niall went to the bar for more orders and Sara got up to dance with an exuberant Harry, who offered to teach her some new moves.

Melody made her excuses, deciding to mingle and catch up with other people she knew and had spotted. She was acutely aware of Catherine's stare as she walked away and felt desperately sorry for Jade, who was left to sit alone and be the butt of Catherine's cruel comments.

★　★　★

Melody tucked her phone away in her handbag and buttoned her coat to the neck. She followed Kieran down to the car deck, with its stench of oil and engine fumes.

The large ramp lowered and the cars streamed out and suddenly they were back on Barradale, in its main town. The herring gulls were swooping across the bay, their grey backs lost in the matching colour of the sea as they cackled like witches' curses on the wind.

Kieran drove with confident care up the winding road from the harbour and turned left towards Marne. It was only a fifteen-minute journey along a narrow coastal road to the seaside village — but it seemed a million miles from Glasgow and Harry and Catherine Sommerlee and Leila's wedding dress.

In a few moments she would be at her parents' house, meeting them and Skye for the first time in a year.

In a strange way, she realised, she was actually glad of Kieran's presence.

He might not like her, but he exuded a certain quiet strength — and she certainly needed all she could get of that right now.

3

'You did it, you brought her home.' Melody's mother hugged her awkwardly, but addressed her remarks to Kieran.

'I would have come without an escort, you know,' Melody protested, uncomfortably aware of Kieran next to her.

'Oh, your dad thought it best,' Maeve Harper said quickly.

Melody's dad winked at her from his seat by the fire. They were all huddled together in the cottage's tiny living room which had never originally been intended to house five adults.

Maeve had pushed Melody and Kieran towards the two-seat sofa and reluctantly she sat beside him, his long leg occasionally brushing against hers in the cramped space. Why it should send a tingle of awareness through her, she had no idea. He had made it abundantly clear that he despised her, and she didn't like him much either for practically kidnapping her and bringing her here to Marne. She gritted her teeth and tried to ignore the sensations.

Skye was sitting opposite on a straight-backed wooden chair brought through from the kitchen. She looked terrible, Melody thought. Her eyes were dark shadowed as if she hadn't slept well in ages and her cheekbones were bruised and red, making her look very unhealthy.

Melody was struck anew by a feeling of being a cuckoo in the nest. Maeve and Skye were both bird-boned and fine-featured with straight, fine, fair hair and small in stature, five foot at most. As a child, Melody had wondered if she was adopted until she met her father's sister, Aunt Rossy, who was even taller than Melody with the same thick, robust auburn hair.

'How was your journey?' Skye blurted out, then flushed and sat on her hands as if they would have given away her secrets. What was it she really wanted to say, Melody wondered — why had her sister brought her all the way here?

'Windy,' she answered and they all laughed, in an unspoken pact to keep everything appearing normal. Or was she imagining the undercurrents, the subtle body language between her parents and her mother's covert surveillance of her younger daughter?

Maeve jumped up and offered tea. Refusing any help, she headed into the kitchen where they could hear the kettle simmering and the clink of porcelain.

'Can you stay for a while?' Skye asked.

Melody ignored Kieran's shifting on the sofa and she nodded.

'A few days, at any rate.'

'Good, I'd like that.' Skye stroked her fingers over her cheeks. Perhaps her skin was as painful as it looked.

Maeve arrived with a tray of cups and saucers and a plate of biscuits. Kieran got up to help her place the tea things on the low table. It was an indication of how often he was here visiting, Melody guessed. He wasn't being treated as a guest, but more like one of the family.

'Kieran, can we take bikes tomorrow? We could take Melody round the coast,' Skye suggested.

It wasn't what Melody expected. If Skye was so desperate to see her that she'd sent Kieran to get her, why was she acting as if Melody was simply here on holiday? Besides . . . cycling? She hadn't been on a bicycle since she was a teenager. It wasn't her sort of thing at all.

But before she could protest or suggest something else, Kieran was answering. 'Sure, no problem. Just turn up tomorrow when you're ready. I'll be able to join you, if it's not too busy.'

Great. So now not only was she expected to get on a bicycle, but Kieran would be coming along too. She'd thought to be rid of him once they got to her parents' house.

Still, she couldn't very well refuse to

go. Looking at Skye's pale face and haunted eyes, it was only right that she follow her sister's lead. At least until she felt ready to talk about why she wanted to see Melody.

Sipping tea from the bone china cup with its pretty matching saucer and sitting there with the painting of the sailboats above the fireplace and the three ducks flying in lucky formation across the wall, it was as if she had never left — never escaped. Nothing had changed in the years since she had last visited this house.

Even then, nothing had been renovated or replaced since she had left home at twenty — and yet her parents didn't seem to notice or mind.

'I haven't had time to completely sort out your old room for you,' Maeve was saying. Her mother sounded nervous. With a shock Melody suddenly realised that this was a big deal for her parents, her coming back home.

Her dad was smiling encouragingly at her. 'Mum's moved some stuff to make room. I'll take your suitcase upstairs and we'll get you settled.'

'No, John, you will not,' Maeve said firmly. 'It's too heavy for you.'

'If you'd let me help you I could've cleared out those old boxes in no time.'

'You know you shouldn't. You're not young any more. You've got to remember that.'

Her father actually looked good for his age. No one would guess he was in his late sixties, Melody thought, but her mother insisted on pampering him. It was ingrained, an instinctive behaviour which her father, for some reason, always went along with. It gave him an easier life, certainly.

'Don't worry, Maeve,' Kieran offered. 'I'll carry Melody's suitcase upstairs.'

Melody followed her mother up the small, crooked cottage staircase, ducking under the low rafters, intensely aware of Kieran behind her, filling the space with his broad shoulders and height.

She stopped at the bedroom door in

dismay. It was a time capsule, a shrine to the teenage Melody. Her old pop posters still hung on the walls and a few dusty school medals lay on the lace mat on her vanity table. There were tea chests of her belongings which she had always meant to send for and never got around to.

'Mum, I thought you were going to ditch all this stuff. Remember we talked about it when I stayed last time?'

'I know, dear. I made a start, but then I just couldn't bring myself to do it. It's still your room and it always will be. I suppose I feel that if I clear your stuff out, it won't be yours any more.'

'Oh, Mum.' Melody hugged her mother impulsively. But the sight of the room still made her spirits sink. It was cramped and cluttered beyond belief. Even as a teenager she had to bow her head when she was in it because of the low slanted attic ceiling. The bed was narrow and single, which she wasn't used to now.

And where would she hang her

clothes? The wardrobe door hung open and she could see that it was crammed with junk.

'I have an empty cottage just now,' Kieran suggested. 'Why doesn't Melody use it while she's here? It's a ten-minute drive at most so she won't be far away.'

Melody was taken aback. Was he really offering to put her up? He must have seen her expression because he added, 'The cottage is in its own grounds so you'll have peace.'

In other words he wouldn't have to bother with her.

'That might be best,' Maeve agreed with an obvious note of relief in her voice.

'Thank you,' Melody said stiffly to Kieran.

Skye waved them off at the door, clearly disappointed that Melody wasn't staying, but with a promise that they would meet the next morning.

They drove in silence away from the coast and up a single track road into the hilly interior of the island. Melody amused herself by imagining what kind of house Kieran had. Judging by his current aura it would be a brooding, towered castle set on a high, fierce mountain.

They turned into a long driveway bordered by early flowering rhododendrons, glorious in crimson and cerise, and attended by the first fat lazy bumble bees of the year, gathering the last pollen before nightfall.

'I'll take you to meet Elspeth first,' Kieran said.

She glanced at his left hand. No ring, but that didn't mean much these days. Elspeth must be his partner or wife. A man like Kieran was unlikely to be single. Not that it mattered anyway, so why had she even thought it?

An impressive stone house came into view ahead. On the doorstep stood a little girl, waving excitedly. Kieran parked a distance away and they crunched over yellow gravel to the house. Kieran picked the girl up in a great swoop and swung her round to Melody.

'This is my beautiful niece, Rona. Say hello, Rona.'

Rona giggled and waved delicate fingers in a greeting. She had elfin features and short curly hair the colour of ripe hay.

'And you must be Melody.' A tall woman appeared at the entrance. 'I'm Kieran's sister, Elspeth. Come away in. Rona, why don't you show Melody into the living room?'

'Kitchen,' Rona stated.

'Living room,' Elspeth repeated.

'Kitchen!'

'Rona doesn't say much but when she does, she likes to have the last word.' Kieran smiled, tousling his niece's head.

The thought suddenly popped into Melody's head that he was gorgeous when he smiled. It was the first time she'd seen him smile since they'd met that morning and it made him younger, more approachable — and, she admitted, more desirable. Not that she did . . . desire him, of course.

Rona beamed up at him and tugged

on Melody's hand.

'I'm suggesting the living room because the kitchen's a mess and not suitable for guests right now,' Elspeth explained, shaking her head at Rona who looked stubbornly back at her.

'I don't mind,' Melody told her, 'if you don't.'

'Kitchen,' Rona grinned, happy again.

Melody let herself be led by the little girl through a wide hallway to a room which was obviously the heart of the home. A massive Aga dominated, alongside which was a clutter of pans and baskets, strings of garlic, a bowlful of onions and a pot of stew simmering away with a wonderful aroma of meat and wine.

An ancient black labrador groaned once at their arrival before flopping its head back down onto its paws and letting out a long, doggy snore.

'Beezer,' Rona announced. She let go of Melody to crouch down and stroke the dog and at her touch, its tail banged on the tiles of the floor.

'Tea, coffee? Or a glass of wine?' Elspeth offered. 'It's late enough to open a bottle, I should think.'

'We can walk to the cottage from here,' Kieran said. 'So a glass of wine is in order. Melody?'

Melody nodded gratefully.

'That would be lovely, thanks. Is the cottage in your garden?'

'We have a cluster of holiday cottages on the estate,' Elspeth explained. 'They're part of the original farm steadings. We run them as a tourism business, along with a bicycle hire shop. I cook evening meals up here at the house for those that want them and I do breakfasts too.'

She sighed worriedly. 'This year has been terrible so far. The weather's been awful and we just haven't had the numbers of people booking that we need. Last year wasn't that great either . . . '

Kieran touched her shoulder reassuringly, 'It'll get better, Ells, it's just a blip. We'll get through, although we may have to come up with some new marketing ideas.'

'Kieran runs the cycle hire and maintains the properties,' Elspeth explained.

'And me!' Rona piped up indignantly.

'Yes, and Rona entertains the guests, don't you, my love? But enough about us. Melody doesn't want to hear about our troubles. How is Skye?'

Actually Melody did want to hear more about Kieran and Elspeth's lives. It put him into context now. He was a landowner in Barradale, rooted here with his sister acting as housekeeper and business partner. Was he single after all? Or did he keep a lover here in Barradale — or perhaps on the mainland? Why should she wonder that at all? It was none of her business.

She zoned back in to Elspeth's enquiring look. 'Skye is . . . to be honest, I don't know how she is. She looks burdened, I guess. Fiona's death has hit her much harder than I ever expected and she hasn't recovered, from what I can see. I'm hoping I'll have a chance to talk to her tomorrow.'

'It'll be good for her, having you here,' Elspeth agreed. 'She's talked of nothing else for the last few weeks — just kept saying, 'I must see Melody'. We thought it odd, given your distance from the family . . . oh!' She stopped in embarrassment, realising what she'd said.

Melody shook her head. 'It's okay, Elspeth, really. I'm not close to Skye and it was a big surprise that she wanted me here. I only hope I can help her before I have to go home again.'

Kieran drained his wine glass and set it down next to Melody's empty glass. 'Come on, I'll show you the cottage,' he said brusquely.

She followed him out into the gathering dusk and they walked down a narrow path scented with mint and other early spring flowers, past a silent lily pond until they reached a white cottage. Beyond there were five more.

'This one's empty so you're welcome to use it,' Kieran said. He pushed open the door and took in her luggage. The cottage was plainly decorated in white, with natural wood skirting and window-sills. Someone, probably Elspeth, had added homely touches, such as a vase of dried flowers and a bookshelf of paperbacks. A collection of seashells lay on the coffee table in the comfortable lounge.

'Rona's been in here again.' Kieran carefully picked up the shells and pocketed them. 'She has the run of the place, so don't get a fright if you hear someone in here. The only place that's out of bounds for her is the pond.'

'Does she go to school locally?' Melody asked curiously. It seemed an isolated sort of play area for a girl of eight or nine.

'She goes to the local primary a couple of days a week. She can't cope with it full-time. She also has a place waiting at a good school on the mainland, but Elspeth can't always spare the time away from the business, so . . . ' He shrugged helplessly.

Changing the subject abruptly, he

asked if she had everything she needed. There was a double bedroom and a single bedroom upstairs along with a small bathroom. Downstairs were a kitchen and lounge and a covered lobby for coats and umbrellas. It was perfect for her needs over the next few days.

She stepped back to give him space to leave and tripped over her suitcase in the hall. Immediately Kieran's arm went round her, holding her and breaking her fall.

She felt the warm strength of his muscular body and the waft of his breath on the top of her hair. He was tall; she didn't know many men taller than her. She was conscious of his lips so close to her. If she turned now and tilted her chin, her lips would touch his. A liquid desire rose in her at his touch and her lips parted unconsciously.

Then like a cold shock of water, he steadied her and pushed her away from him. Without a word he nodded curtly and left, closing the cottage door firmly with a click.

Melody's legs were trembling and her mind racing at what had just happened, at her body's betrayal. She knew in her head that the last thing she wanted was to have anything to do with Kieran Matthews, but her body was telling a different story.

4

He had left quickly because he had to. Another moment and he would have kissed her. It was madness. She was all the things he despised in a woman, and yet he wanted her anyway.

He had even felt sorry for her at the Harpers' house, staring into the miserably small bedroom with no room to swing the proverbial cat, let alone accommodate a tall woman like Melody. Her dismay had triggered his offer of the holiday cottage.

So much for vowing to have nothing more to do with her once they reached Marne. And to top it all, he was going cycling with her around the island. In this at least he could defend himself; he had done it for Skye. He'd grown fond of her in a big brotherly way since he had met the Harpers, and protected her when he felt it necessary.

Although Skye wanted Melody here, it was potentially awkward since they didn't know each other well. Perhaps, Kieran reasoned, if he was around he could mediate if needed. Often a third person eased conversation and kept it flowing between two people who weren't sure of each other.

* * *

The next morning, Kieran opened up the bicycle hire shop on the estate and began to gather what they would need and check the bikes' condition. It was superfluous, really; he kept them in very good order as a matter of course, and prided himself that he'd never yet had a dissatisfied customer or a bike returned with complaints.

He tightened the gears on one bike and turned it towards the entrance of the shop . . . and there she was. The woman who had entered his confused dreams and kept him restless all night.

She was dressed in a simple flowered

dress which hugged her in all the right places, a pair of tall pink sandals and with an oversized handbag slung over her shoulder.

'Have you brought a change of clothes?' he asked, simultaneously admiring her look while irritated at its frivolity.

'No.' She looked down, her hair loose and falling forward to shade her face. 'Why?'

'You can't cycle in that,' Kieran stated. 'Come up to the house and borrow something of Elspeth's. She's about the same size as you. You should tie your hair back, too.'

'Sorry,' Melody answered, unexpectedly grinning at him. 'I should've thought about it. I haven't been on a bike in years. I had a vision of drifting lazily through lanes, not mountain biking.'

His heart gave a lurch. She was even more attractive with that grin showing perfect white teeth and creating an irresistible dimple in her left cheek.

'The terrain's rocky and bumpy. We'll need proper mountain bikes.' Did he have to sound so pompous, even to himself? Her grin disappeared and he focused on polishing the bike's frame which was already gleaming.

'Well, I'll go and see Elspeth. Skye should be here soon. Please tell her where I am.'

He nodded, cursing himself. She had retreated into a formal tone with him again and he couldn't blame her. He wanted to see her smile again.

Skye arrived shortly after Melody had gone up to the house. 'Hey. I'm looking forward to this. I've brought a picnic that Mum's made for us. Shall I put it in the panniers?'

'You're spoilt, you know that?' Kieran teased. 'Getting your mum to make the lunch.'

'She loves doing it,' Skye protested.

'Just as well then,' he shot back, and she laughed easily.

Melody returned sooner than he expected, and now she was clad in jeans and trainers with a thin purple fleece top and her hair pulled back into a ponytail. She was still beautiful.

'Much better,' he said approvingly, giving them a bike each.

Skye mounted hers with the ease of someone who was used to cycling often.

Kieran waited to watch Melody in case she needed help. She swung her leg over gingerly and balanced with the tips of her toes on the ground.

'Ready?' he called, and they set off, Kieran at the front, Skye in the middle and Melody slowly bringing up the rear.

They cycled down the long driveway and onto the single track road. In a car one was hardly aware of the contours of the terrain, but on a bike every gradient was felt, especially in the thigh muscles. After a time they joined the coastal road and were able to make use of an old path that paralled the road and allowed spectacular views of the foamy sea, sculpted by the breeze and the rocky shoreline of Barradale.

'Okay?' Kieran shouted back over the wind.

Skye waved an okay back. Melody

didn't answer and he realised it was because she was concentrating hard on staying on the bicycle. She was biting her lip and frowning intensely, while the wind blew against them, forcing them to work their legs even harder to get where they wanted to go. She wasn't moaning or complaining, which surprised him; she was just getting on with it as best she could.

They rounded a long curve in the path and arrived at a sandy bay. Kieran stopped expertly, Skye slewed round beyond him to drop her bike and run onto the sand. Melody flew past him at speed with a scream and toppled over Skye's bike.

'Melody!' Kieran sprang to the tumble of bikes and legs and arms and pulled her gently free. She groaned.

'Are you all right? Is anything broken?'

He felt a crackle of electricity at the touch of her skin.

'Just bruised,' Melody said, still holding his hand as she trembled with after-shock. She laughed shakily. 'But my dignity's definitely broken.'

'Do you make a habit of falling over?' Kieran asked huskily, remembering the feel of her body from when he had steadied her last night. She blushed and released his hand. So she had felt it too; the tingle of excitement when they touched.

Her hand was cut and she took out a fresh paper hankie to mop a trickle of blood.

'You're a good sport,' he found himself saying — and he meant it. Perhaps she had hidden depths after all.

'Because you expected me to complain selfishly all the way here?' Melody squinted up at him as she dabbed at her hand.

Now it was his turn to redden, because yes, he had expected that and no more from her.

'You're brave, too,' he admitted. He was beginning to admire her, albeit reluctantly.

'That must have hurt you more than my hand hurts me,' Melody commented drily.

He looked at her but she was grinning despite a residue of tears in the corners of her eyes from the fall.

He found himself grinning back. 'Come on, let me patch up your hand from the first aid kit and then we can join Skye out on the promontory.'

'Fair enough, but let's leave the bikes. I can see there's a little path we could cycle out on, but right now I'd prefer to walk.'

Skye was sitting on a stone outcrop looking out at the wild sea when they found her. She was oblivious to the accident and immediately concerned for Melody when she saw the large sticking plaster on her hand, until Melody related the tale with such self-deprecating wit that she had them both laughing.

The sweet smell of coconut from the gorse petals wafted towards them and everywhere the brown-pink ball blossoms of last year's sea thrift bobbed and swayed in nooks in the craggy rocks. The sea roared exuberantly and dashed itself uncaringly against the outcrop far below them.

'Do you remember this place?' Skye asked Melody.

'Not really.' There was a hint of familiarity about it but Melody had spent so many years suppressing her memories of Barradale that sometimes they were impossible to resurrect.

'You don't remember cycling here with Mum and Dad when we were teenagers?' Skye persisted. 'Once you were so angry over something that you threw your bike off the cliff! Dad had to retrieve it when the tide went out. They didn't even tell you off. I never understood why they were so calm with you over it.'

'I do recall my bike being mangled. Gosh, so that was here on this very spot? I'd forgotten that. The bike was never the same again, even though Dad did his best to mend it. What a horrible teenager I must have been to live with.'

'You were horrible. I'm sorry to have to tell you the truth of that but you were always so angry and I was scared of your moods, so I kept my distance as

61

much as I could. I think that's why we never clicked because I was always avoiding you.'

Melody was truly horrified at Skye's quiet words. She reached out and laid her hand on her sister's arm.

'I'm so sorry, Skye, I really am. I had no idea that was what you were doing. I've always thought we weren't close because we were different personalities, but actually it was all my fault.'

There was a silence between them, filled only by the rasp of the waves and the mournful cry of a far off seabird.

Kieran wondered if this was what Skye had wanted to tell Melody. Was this the reason he had dragged Melody from Glasgow? He sensed it wasn't the whole story yet.

To break the silence he asked a question himself.

'Why were you so angry?'

'Teenagers have a lot of natural anger anyway, don't they? But Skye's right, it was more than that. I only wish I'd known then how it would affect my relationship with my only sister.' She paused, clearly emotional.

Kieran felt the strongest impulse to cuddle and comfort her, to erase her sadness with his strength. But he couldn't, of course. He could only sit and listen.

'It was my fault too,' Skye said before Melody could continue. 'When Mum and Dad found out I was being bullied at school in Glasgow, they decided it would be better for all of us to move here. I think they wanted to downsize anyway and it gave them the reason to do so. I was very happy with the move here but you lost out, didn't you?'

'I had to leave all my friends and the school I loved. I hated Barradale and for a long time, yes, I was incredibly angry with Mum and Dad for ripping me from my life,' Melody confessed. 'Let's be honest, I never settled here. I vowed to return to the mainland and live my own life as soon as I was old enough.'

'So that's why you were so unhappy

at returning here with me,' Kieran said slowly. 'Barradale holds too many bad memories for you. It's true that island life isn't for everyone.'

He found himself thinking of Sophie when he said it. It was true that Barradale most certainly hadn't suited her at all.

'The funny thing is that now I'm back this time, it's not so bad,' Melody remarked, as if she had just realised this. 'I suppose I know that I can leave again, any time.' She paused a moment before turning to Skye and adding, 'And I'm determined to spend time with you, Skye. I don't know if I can make it up to you for being such a grouch all those years but I'd like to try.'

Skye looked strangely uncomfortable. She opened her mouth as if to say something but at that moment her hat blew off her head and then they were all running back down the path after it while a capricious breeze lifted it and bowled it along.

'The thing is,' Skye said, finally grabbing her hat just as they reached the bikes, 'this is the first time in a long while that I've actually felt happy.' She paused and concentrated on folding the hat's rim neatly all the way round before continuing, 'But at the same time I feel guilty for it, you know . . . guilty for laughing and running and cycling and . . . and for being alive when Fiona's not.' Her knuckles whitened as she gripped her hat.

'It's not your fault, any of it. It was a horrible, freak accident,' Melody told her gently.

'I know that in my head,' Skye explained. 'But my heart and my instincts tell me otherwise. It feels wrong to be enjoying myself when my best friend can't.'

'It's been over a year. Fiona wouldn't want you to be mourning this long,' Kieran said gently.

'I'm sure you're right,' Skye admitted, still folding her hat until now it resembled a stiff, corrugated fan. 'But I can't shake it, and it's made me realise how suddenly life can change.

'Did you know she phoned me just before she left that day? She was so excited to be going climbing on a new route . . . and then she never came home. I keep thinking how it could happen to me, too. I don't mean climbing since I don't do stuff like that, but something could happen to me — anything, an accident maybe — and I would be gone before I could put things right.'

Melody and Kieran both looked at her in silent concern. Kieran glanced then at Melody to say wordlessly, *This is what I meant; this is why you had to come home.*

She looked back at him with her wide hazel eyes, then turned back to Skye. 'What do you mean about putting things right?' she asked her sister, but Skye shook her head.

She released her tight grasp on her hat and it bounced back, hat-shaped once more. Skye jammed it on her head and pulled her bike upright. She smiled at them.

'Come on. Don't look so worried, you two. I'll be okay. I just need more time to work it out. And it's good having you here, Melody.'

With that they had to be content.

They cycled slowly back to the estate, each caught in their own thoughts. What was Melody thinking? Kieran wondered. Was she focused on Skye or was she further back in time, remembering herself as an unhappy and resentful teenager out of place in Barradale and taking it out on everyone else? He didn't blame her. Knowing a bit more about her background explained her reluctance to return to the island. She was a more complex person than he had given her credit for.

With a mental jolt that coincided perfectly with a physical jerk as his wheel went into a pothole in the road, he realised he was more intrigued by her now and that he couldn't simply write her off as shallow and selfish.

A red danger sign flashed past them as they cycled along, a warning of the recent small landslide on the edge of the hill. But it could have been put up just for him; there was danger in thinking about Melody Harper. She was so similar to Sophie in many ways. How could he be foolish enough to go down that particular path again? Hadn't he experienced enough pain?

The landslide was chained off with a secure metal link fence to prevent access. He had thought of his heart that way for a long time; locked off, secure and safe. He couldn't let a woman like Melody be the one to break inside.

5

Elspeth smoothed her hands down the front of her dress nervously. 'I'm suddenly not sure this is a good idea after all. What if no one comes?'

Behind her, stacked along the kitchen worktops, were plates of cakes, tins of muffins, a layer of tray bakes and a centrepiece of a chocolate fountain, all ready to go.

Melody's mouth watered. The air was scented with vanilla, almonds and sugar. Rona's eyes were wide like saucers at the sight of so much delicious food.

'It's going to be great,' Melody soothed. She pulled a flyer from her jeans pocket and looked at it again. ' 'Open Day at Aucher Estate. Food stalls, cycling, guided walks, face-painting and more.' That's bound to grab people's attention. I love the artwork, too.'

'I did the shapes and colours,' Rona

said, her little face bright with pride.

'Did you? Well, they're fantastic,' Melody told her, meaning it. The shapes were simple but satisfyingly organic and flowing while the bold primary colours caught the eye.

'Rona's really good at art,' Elspeth said, kissing the top of her daughter's head. 'That's partly why I want her to go to the school on the mainland. It's got an amazing art department and I just know she'd love it.'

'Maybe you could get some help here? That would give you more time to get Rona to the mainland and back on the ferry.'

'It's a lovely idea, but at the moment we're struggling to make a profit on the estate at all. Which brings us neatly back to today's Open Day.' Elspeth laughed. 'Fingers crossed it drums up some new business and fills those empty cottages. Now, Melody, would you help me shift these cakes out to the stalls? I think Kieran should be set up and ready by now.'

Melody felt a little lift in her spirits at the sound of his name. It was ridiculous, like a schoolgirl with her first serious crush. She felt an anticipation at seeing him again so soon, the cycle trip a few days ago still fresh in her mind. She helped Elspeth load up with baking produce and then carefully filled another tray for herself to carry.

'Thanks for inviting me along today with Mum and Dad and Skye,' she said when she got outside.

'Don't be daft, you're very welcome. Besides, you're staying in the cottage. If it gets busy you'll be stuck right in the middle of it all as it is. Also I had another cunning reason — I needed an extra pair of hands.'

'Oh, well — if I'd known you just wanted a slave, I'd have cried off,' Melody teased with mock anger. She felt very at ease with Elspeth, as if she'd known her a long time.

'Too late now. Come on, slave, let's get the food laid out. Thank goodness it's a dry day.'

'Warm too.' Melody was wearing a blouse she had designed and created herself in chocolate and lime cotton with slashed sleeves and a low neck. Rona had been mesmerised by it, stroking the material and saying how much she liked the buttons. Melody was particularly pleased with the buttons, which were all different and each an antique from a London flea market she had visited during a fashion week the previous year. It was nice to be able wear the blouse and show it off, minus layers of jackets and woollens for the weather.

Her heart squeezed. Kieran was finishing putting up the trestle tables not far from the cluster of pine trees. He looked strong and fit and tanned in his jeans and blue shirt. He turned at the sound of their chatter and smiled at them.

I wish he would smile only for me. A crazy impulsive thought. He wasn't for her. She still didn't know if he had a partner, a lover. Maybe she would meet her and be introduced to her today. It soured her mood, taking the sun behind a small, mean cloud.

Elspeth frowned worriedly at the sky. Kieran looked keenly at Melody, ready to speak, but Maeve Harper bustled up, her arms full of Cellophane-wrapped parcels.

Mum, your timing is terrible, Melody thought to herself.

'Kieran!' she called out. 'I've brought some home baking. Where do you want it?'

He turned solicitously to her mother and the great array of goodies being offered. Melody's dad came slowly up the path to join them, too.

'Hello love,' he said as he approached. 'Your mother's overdone it in her enthusiasm, I'm afraid. The oven's burnt out with the effort.'

Melody pulled over the fold-out chair for him. It was like a Pavlovian response to her father — they all did it; wherever they went, they got him chairs, made him sit, encouraged him to be still.

They didn't even question it, just copied Maeve's concern.

Did her father even want a seat? He did sit, heavily, and was content to watch the frenzied activity.

But Melody had lost her chance and Kieran had gone in the direction of the cottages. One of them was being opened up today as a showhouse and Melody guessed he was checking that everything was perfect and in place.

'Skye's not coming today,' John Harper said.

'Why not? Is she still sick?'

'She's feeling poorly. She said she might join us later.'

'Is she often sick? She was fine when we went cycling but I know she's been off colour the last couple of days, that's why I've haven't been round. I didn't want to bother her.'

'Since Fiona's accident her health hasn't been one hundred percent,' her dad explained. He pursed his lips and blew out strongly. In that instant Melody saw him as an old man with his thinning grey hair, saggy jowls and lined forehead. It gave her a pang of panic. Time was rolling on faster and faster, only she hadn't noticed it before. It was as if time had speeded up more on Barradale than at home in Glasgow.

'Are you okay, Dad?'

'Me?' He sounded faintly surprised. 'I don't think it's catching, love. No, Skye gets bugs easily. Her immune system's low, she gets a lot of tummy bouts.' He paused, let the silence draw out between them, then added plainly, 'I'm glad you've come home, Melody.'

He coughed and rubbed an imaginary fleck from the knee of his trousers. For her father, that was as emotional as it got. She knew better than to try to hug him or discuss it further.

'I think I'll go and freshen up before the gates open.'

Great idea, Melody. Because you know perfectly well who'll be there at the cottage.

★　★　★

She found him hammering a sign onto a stake at the open cottage and stopped to admire the flex of his arm muscles. He stopped mid-swing when he saw her and laid the hammer down.

'Melody.' Even the dark velvet of his voice made her spine tingle, even though she tried not to let it.

'Kieran. I'm just — ' *Just what? Just coincidentally here with you under a breezy, inviting sky.*

'Thanks for helping Elspeth out with the Open Day. I really appreciate it. We both do.'

'Don't mention it. I hope today's a success and I'm happy to help.' *Especially if it means being around you.*

What was the matter with her today? There was something in the air, some madness of spirit, but was it just for her? His eyes darkened and he reached for her.

This is it, Melody thought. *He's going to kiss me and I'm going to let him.* His hand went up to her hair and came away with a pine twig. Melody let out her caught breath, along with a hefty dose of disappointment.

'Sorry. Couldn't let you walk around with half of an Aucher tree in your hair.' He smiled.

'Thanks,' she said feebly. 'I'm just going to get tidied up, then I'll help up at the marquee.'

Her hands were trembling and she clasped one to the other, amazed at the physical effect he could have on her, and turned to see Elspeth, laden with bags and watching her with an unreadable expression.

'Kieran, the truck's arrived with the tables and chairs from the marquee. I wasn't sure if you wanted to take charge of it?'

'Will do. This sign's ready, so I'll see you two back up at the house,' he said, turning to leave.

Elspeth waited until he was out of sight then handed Melody a pile of freshly laundered soft towels.

'Maybe you'll help me put these in the show house?'

The open cottage was immaculate, with its wooden sills and furniture waxed and the surfaces gleaming. An enticing scent of lavender pervaded the air; Elspeth had added a vase of pansies to the table and laid out mats as though an inviting meal was being prepared in the adjacent tiny kitchen.

'I like this cottage best,' Elspeth said suddenly.

'Why's that? It's really nicely set up but aren't the cottages all very similar?'

'This is where I first lived when my marriage ended.'

'Oh, I'm sorry.' Melody wasn't sure what to say. She refolded an already folded towel.

'No, that came out wrong. It wasn't a messy divorce, although it had the same financial effect. My husband died, you see. But once I had recovered from the shock of it, I received another body blow — he had gambled away our life savings without telling me.'

'Oh, that's awful,' Melody murmured, aghast.

'I had no idea he gambled. When I first met him he never so much as spent a penny on risks, never showed any interest in the horse races or arcade machines or anything of the sort.'

'What did he gamble on?'

'Internet casinos. The funny thing is that it was me that insisted on buying a computer and on getting connected to the web. Ironically I never really got the hang of it, while he ended up surfing most evenings. I thought he was working, but now I know he was actually playing virtual cards and rolling dice while getting deeper and deeper into debt.'

'What on earth did you do?'

'At first I didn't know what I was going to do. Rona was only small and suddenly there I was, a widow at thirty with no money and nowhere to live, once they repossessed the house.'

'So you ended up here with Kieran?'

'Not immediately. This cottage belonged to an old Barradale family who owned Aucher Estate at the time — the Mackinnons. Jamie Mackinnon was a cousin of sorts to my husband and he kindly let me stay here until I sorted myself out.'

'So where was Kieran?'

'He was still in Europe running his holiday business. When he heard what had happened he sold up and moved back here.'

'Back? Were you always from Barradale, then?'

'No, we're from Ireland originally but we spent most of our family summer holidays as kids here. That's how I met Don, my husband, when I worked summers here as a teenager.'

The towels were neat and beautifully displayed, the duvet straightened and the curtains artfully scalloped to let in the bright day. Melody sat on the bed next to Elspeth and listened.

'Anyway, Jamie Mackinnon was selling up so Kieran bought the estate for us to run together as a business and to provide me and Rona with a secure home and a future.'

'So it all worked out in the end,' Melody said lamely. She was getting it now, the sub-text. Kieran was devoted to his sister and his niece. He was tied to Barradale as surely as if he had been born and bred here and he was never going to leave it.

If she had thought before that Kieran wasn't for her, she was certain of it now, thanks to Elspeth's story. Which was no doubt why she had told it. It was a gentle but firm warning not to mess with her brother's affections. Clearly it wasn't just brother-protecting-sister here, but worked equally both ways.

'We should go back to the house.' Elspeth smiled. 'I've left Rona alone long enough. She'll be following Kieran around like a puppy wanting attention.' Her voice was back to its usual cheerful vigour and Melody realised thankfully that the warning was finished. But not forgotten.

'I can see he's devoted to her,' Melody said, relieved they were back on a friendly footing.

Elspeth gathered the empty bags which had held the towels and gave the bed coverings a last, unnecessary straighten.

'Yes, he's fantastic with her. He was keen to have kids himself at one stage, but of course Sophie wouldn't hear of it.'

'Is that his partner?' Melody felt sick, then chastised herself for being silly. He was gorgeous, so of course he wasn't single.

'His ex-wife. Look, I shouldn't have told you that, so please don't mention it to Kieran. It's not my story to tell.'

Melody agreed and politely changed the subject to the opening of the event, which then had them both hurrying up the path to the house to be there on time.

There was a gala atmosphere. The sun had struggled out again from behind tough little clouds and the day was unseasonably warm. There were already twenty or so visitors wandering about curiously. Some people were buying home baking at the stalls where Melody noticed her mother, happy and in her element, describing ingredients and flavours to whichever customers would listen.

Inside the large marquee there were information stalls from different organisations invited along for the day. There were animal charities, waste recycling and activity holiday companies along with a gathering point for guided walks of the estate which were to be held by Kieran himself. A loud horn signalled the arrival of a tourist bus from the mainland.

'I'm glad to see they've arrived at last.' Kieran's voice sounded behind her.

Melody turned to him. 'There must be fifty or a hundred people there.'

'I negotiated this stop for them on their tour of the island,' Kieran told her. 'Listen, can you keep an eye on Rona for me until I'm finished with this lot?'

'Of course.'

He touched her lightly on the shoulder in thanks, leaving a burning spot. She had to stop this! She had been warned off, hadn't she? But even if she hadn't been, it was futile. He was here and in a matter of days, she would be back at home in Glasgow, all being well. Why couldn't her body understand that?

A sudden shrill cry split the air. Melody was startled from her unhelpful thoughts to see Rona red-faced and stamping her foot on the ground in front of her mother. People were looking round as Elspeth desperately grabbed at her daughter. Rona slipped easily from her mother's grasp and ran out the far side of the marquee just as Melody caught up with Elspeth.

'What happened?'

Elspeth shook her head, her lips tight. 'She wants to go and find Kieran. I've told her she can't because he's taken the bus load on a guided walk on the other side of the estate woodlands. I should go after her.'

Melody stopped her. 'No — why not let me go and talk to her? You're needed here to co-ordinate the day, aren't you?'

Elspeth nodded unhappily. 'Thanks, Melody.'

Melody hurried from the marquee wishing she hadn't worn her high rope wedge sandals. They weren't designed for running on hummocky grass. Luckily Rona hadn't gone far. She was sitting hunched up, hugging her knees, on a little hummock under the pine trees. Her face was set in a scowl.

Melody sat beside her and together they looked down at the busy scene as people enjoyed the event. A hand stole out and stroked the fabric of Melody's blouse. It gave her an idea — a way of distracting Rona and cheering her up.

'Would you like to see my book of fabric samples?' she offered tentatively.

'What book?'

'Do you have a scrapbook?' Melody asked.

'Yes. Me and Mummy glue pictures there.'

'Well I have a scrapbook, too, but instead of cutting pictures from magazines, I glue in bits of materials. They give me ideas for clothing I could make.'

'Where is it?' The scowl was gone, cleared as if by magic, instantly replaced with an expectant happiness.

'At my cottage. Come on, I'll show you.'

They threaded their way down the path, Rona holding Melody's hand trustingly. It felt strange but nice. She didn't know any children. None of the gang had babies or any intention of having any as they would most definitely interfere with their fledgling careers. She and Skye had cousins with kids, but there wasn't a close enough connection to keep in touch.

It was novel being here with Rona, and surprisingly fun. They reached the cottage, skirting the forbidden pond and Melody closed the door with relief on the crowd's gabble outside. It sounded as though the show house cottage next door was a real success. She wondered briefly whether the towels had retained their fluffy, folded perfection.

'Hurry up, Melody!' Rona ordered, bouncing on the sofa and making it creak alarmingly.

Melody obediently fetched her fabric sample book and poured a glass of juice for her guest. Together they pored over the materials and Melody described them and how she imagined she might use them. Rona listened politely but her fingers were busy on texture and feel, her eyes flickering on the vivid colours and patterns — and she was even smelling the swatches as if they held delicate perfumes in their cotton and silk strands.

'I like these,' she pronounced finally.

'Yes, I can see that,' Melody agreed, smiling. 'You can come here any time and look at them, okay?'

Rona nodded contentedly.

The door opened and Kieran appeared, looking worried. His face relaxed when he saw the two of them sitting together.

'Hey, beautiful.' For a crazy moment Melody hoped he meant her, but then he hunkered down to Rona's level. 'Are you being good, then?'

'She's been great,' Melody said quickly, in case his question reminded Rona of her earlier annoyance at not being allowed to follow him into the woodlands.

'Melody's book,' Rona said.

'Book?'

'It's a fabric sample book,' Melody explained, showing it to him. 'For keeping notes and designs.' Their fingers touched briefly as she passed it over to him. *Forget it.*

'This is great.' Kieran glanced at her warmly over the leaves of the open book. 'It was really good of you to spend time with my naughty niece here.' He flicked one of Rona's curls teasingly and she giggled and squirmed. 'You have to say sorry to your mum for being bad-tempered,' he said, trying to be stern.

Rona wasn't taken in but nodded obligingly. 'Sorry, Mum.'

'To her face, Rona. She's at the house, so why don't you go now and tell her? Beezer needs a cuddle, too — he's not been for his walk today.'

Rona ran to the cottage door, hesitated, then ran back and gave Melody a short but fierce hug before running off again.

'You're honoured.' Kieran laughed. 'She only ever hugs me, Elspeth and Beezer.'

Melody was flooded with sudden hot confusion. He filled the tiny cottage with his broad shoulders and long legs. She could smell his scent, masculine skin and plain soap.

She backed off a little in the direction of the kitchen. 'Coffee?'

'Sure. I could use a break from the guiding. The next one isn't until two-thirty.'

He followed her into the even smaller kitchen. *Move back!* She concentrated on making the coffee. She could manage that, couldn't she? Pour water into the kettle and flick the switch to boil it. Two scoops of rich, black grains trailing like soil into the glass cafetière.

Now add the hot water and let the aromatic steam rise. Steep for three minutes, enough time to gather two mugs and a small jug of milk. And every second an awareness of him behind her, making the little hairs stand up on the back of her neck in readiness.

'Here, I'll take these for you.'

She turned with the mugs almost into his embrace. His dark blue eyes gazed directly into hers and she watched his Adam's apple move in his throat as he swallowed. She felt unexpectedly nervous and at the same time improbably excited.

'Melody . . . '

The terrible crass jingle of a well-known pop tune rent the air between them. Kieran's arms dropped to his sides as Melody slipped past him, muttering about her mobile phone.

'Darling, are you surviving out there in the boonies?' Harry's casual voice sounded tinny. The reception for mobile phones on Barradale really wasn't great.

'It's not the back of beyond, you

know, Harry,' she retorted, then wondered why she was being defensive. Harry knew how much she hated Barradale; goodness knows she had told him so many times over the years.

'Not the back of beyond? Ha ha, good joke. No really. I'm missing you, sweetie. I was hoping you'd be back by now. Didn't you promise me some designs for an article I'm writing? I'm running out of ideas right now.'

So that was it. Harry wasn't actually missing *her*. He was missing her artistic input into his writing and photography. It was typical of Harry. Something else struck her.

'How did you know I was here, anyway? I was going to phone and tell you but I couldn't get reception.'

'I met a mad woman, Leila something — Pigeon? Hawks? Anyway she was with Cath at the wedding show in Manchester and she mentioned it then that you were on the island. You missed quite a show — the fabrics were wonderful and Cath's new collection was fabulous. I got an exclusive on it.'

Melody barely listened as Harry described Catherine Sommerlee's latest dresses. What was Leila Doves doing in the company of Catherine, anyway? It didn't make any sense. She tried to zone back in to Harry's conversation. He was still in full flow and she hadn't been missed at all at her end of the phone.

'So the upshot is that we are all frazzled here because the Manchester show was so fab. How can we compete? So I suggested a mini-break and Niall and Sara were totally up for it. It'll freshen our creativity and we'll come back revitalised and ready for our own show.'

'Where are you going to?' Melody dreaded his answer because she knew suddenly exactly where they were going.

'We're coming to visit you, darling.'

'I'm not sure that's a good idea, Harry.'

'Of course it is. We're all missing you

and we're curious to visit your quaint little island. It might even inspire us with new themes for next season.'

She didn't want them here, her gut instinct told her that. But why would she not want her best friends around? Melody's emotions tumbled like balls in a washer, but before she could sort them out Harry was speaking again. 'It's all sorted. We're booked on the morning ferry on Saturday. See you then!'

The phone clicked off. She dropped it unceremoniously onto the sofa, then noticed the two coffee mugs on the low table. Kieran had gone.

★   ★   ★

She replayed it in her mind, puzzled as to why he had abandoned her so quickly. Then her heart sank. He had almost reached for her, seemed about to say something important when her phone had rung. He had hung about until she mentioned Harry's name.

Then he had quietly put down the mugs and she had stupidly been distracted by the mention of Catherine Sommerlee and Leila Doves.

She should have signalled to him to stay. Should have signalled — how? — that Harry was just a friend, that she wanted him to please stay, to please reconnect to whatever had happened between them in the kitchen, but it was too late.

Melody poured herself a cup of cold coffee and drank it miserably. Harry, Niall and Sara were coming to Barradale and she could do nothing to prevent it.

6

The sparks from the burning cherry logs flew like fireflies against the black sky. A myriad of stars twinkled, and the air was mild and cosy like a warm wrap.

Melody, Kieran and Elspeth sat around the brazier enjoying the heat of the fire. Around them lay the remains of the community barbecue which had been the grand finale to the day. Forty or more people had stayed to the end to tuck into venison sausages and burgers along with vegetable kebabs, soft flour-dusted rolls and huge trays of salad.

The Harpers had left with the last of the crowd and Rona had gone to bed, asleep almost instantly as her head hit the pillow. Beezer lay at the foot of the bed guarding her as he did faithfully every evening, snoring gently and wagging his tail occasionally as he hunted dream rabbits.

'Another burger, Melody?' Elspeth asked, finishing up what was on her own plate of food and lining her cutlery up neatly ready for washing.

They had all eaten considerably later than their visitors, making sure that everyone at the barbecue was satisfied with their food and had a place to sit and company to sit with.

'Thanks, but I think I'd burst if I ate another thing,' Melody groaned, patting her tummy.

'A glass of wine will help settle you,' Kieran suggested, pouring each of them a generous measure of the ruby liquid. 'I think we deserve to celebrate because my gut feeling is that today was a roaring success. Bookings for the cottages have soared, and in fact they're now block booked until Easter! The bicycle hire is on the up, too and I had groups telling me they're definitely coming back next weekend to explore the woodlands and the hills.'

'Do you own the hills beyond the woods?' Melody asked, accepting the glass of wine.

'Sadly no, but there are some good sized mountains on Barradale and we get hill walkers all year round climbing them.'

Beside the fire, Elspeth gave a loud yawn. 'Sorry,' she said, trying to stifle another one, 'I'm exhausted. I'm going to have to break up the party and head for bed.'

'I should go too,' Melody said.

'Stay a bit longer and help me finish this bottle,' Kieran said.

It was awkward. Melody knew she wanted to, but also that she shouldn't really. The vibe from Elspeth was that the party was finished and it was time for them, all three, to disperse.

Yet again she was trying to protect her brother — but from what, really? Melody's mind reasoned that there was nothing going on between her and Kieran, and many good reasons why there shouldn't be. What could be wrong with sitting by the fire and sipping a glass of wine with a friend? For he had at least become that, she reckoned. His initial hostility when he met her in Glasgow had gone ever since their cycling trip and there was an easiness between them. She neatly ignored the fact that there was tension too, of a physical nature.

'Okay, why not? Another glass of wine would be lovely.' She picked up another log and set it on the brazier where sweet cherry smoke wafted out and bright jewels of fire appeared, cracking open the wood in a satisfying manner.

'Good night then.' Elspeth smiled at them both, her eyes puffy with weariness.

They waved to her as she went into the house and then sat quietly together for a while simply watching the bright fire and feeling its welcome heat on their skin.

'She likes you a lot,' Kieran remarked. 'It's good for her to find a girl friend — she spends too much time alone or with only me and Rona.'

'I really like Elspeth too.' Melody was warmed by his comment. 'I'm glad I met her. But in a few days I'll be back in Glasgow, which won't help much if she's lonely here.'

'Perhaps you could keep in touch,' Kieran suggested. 'Who knows, maybe you'll even visit Barradale again.' There was a teasing note in his voice now and Melody risked a glance at him away from her view of the mesmeric fire.

He was grinning at her and raised his glass for a toast. 'To Melody Harper and to her next visit to the back of beyond.'

She set her glass down and looked at him more seriously. 'You heard that, did you? When I was talking to Harry.'

Kieran put his own glass down on the slabs next to the brazier. 'Yes, I'm sorry. I couldn't help overhearing a bit of your conversation before I left.'

'Why did you leave? We were going to have coffee together and then I turned round and you'd gone.' As she said it she sounded pathetic even to herself.

'I felt it was rude to eavesdrop. Harry sounded like someone special.' He shrugged as if to say it was no big deal. Which it wasn't, but Melody was suddenly irritated. He'd given up awfully quickly, melting away like that — especially since she'd had the sense he was going to say something of import to her.

'Harry's a friend, that's all.' Then her irrational irritation was replaced by gloom as she remembered the outcome of that particular conversation.

'What is it?' Kieran asked softly. 'You've got a frown line on your forehead.' He reached out and stroked her forehead, one gentle touch so quickly gone, but she could feel the whorl of his fingertip like a brand above her eyes.

'It's nothing, not really.' She shook her head, her thick auburn hair falling forward, thankfully covering her too-mobile face. 'My friends are coming over next weekend to visit me.'

'Well, that's a good thing, isn't it? It also means that your few days here will have turned into a week or more, which means Elspeth will have the pleasure of your company for longer.'

And what do you feel? Will my company please you, too? Melody wondered.

'Unfortunately I can't offer them any holiday accommodation at Aucher now that the cottages are fully booked for the next few months,' Kieran continued.

Melody couldn't begin to imagine Harry or Niall or Sara staying in one of the cottages. She cringed inwardly at what they would say if it was offered. *Hicksville, darling. Backwoods. Where's the underfloor heating?* No, it would never do. If only they weren't coming in the first instance.

'I expect they'll book into Barradale Hotel,' she said swiftly.

She pulled her chair closer to the fire feeling a chill as the night thickened around them. The fire, too, was greying with ash and softened embers and no longer giving out the same level of searing heat. It spat occasionally where fire met wood sap, puffing up ash where it fell, then like sporadic dark snow-flakes onto her hair and clothes and onto the ground.

Kieran drew his chair up too, so that their knees were almost touching as they sought the last of the heat.

'So are these friends from your work?' Kieran asked.

'From college.' Melody explained how she and Harry, Niall and Sara had met and how their ambitions were tied together creatively and mutually bound to the future. When she stopped there was a silence. An owl hooted eerily. She imagined it gliding on dark wings over the moors on its deadly mission.

'So you really have created a new life for yourself, quite separate from your family and from Barradale,' was Kieran's only comment when she'd finished.

She searched for a note of criticism but wasn't sure if it really was there or not.

'I had to,' she said simply. 'I was dying there. I knew if I didn't get out then, that I never would.' It was suddenly vital to her that he got it, that he understood her deep-rooted fear of being buried alive in this place where she had been so desperately unhappy.

'It isn't so bad a place.' Kieran spread his hands as if to encompass all of their surroundings. The big, old stone house so solid and reassuring, the neatly cut lawns, the scattered steadings and the backdrop of hill ranges and forest.

'Maybe not for you. You chose to come back.'

She felt suddenly frustrated that she couldn't describe properly to him just how it had been for her at the age of eighteen.

'I came back because I had to,' Kieran corrected her, his blue eyes serious as he met her gaze steadily. 'Elspeth was in a lot of trouble at the time, Melody, and she needed me, as did Rona. So I made a conscious decision to fold up my life in France and come back here. It was my duty to my family.'

Duty. Family. Words he had thrown

at her and accused her of not caring about, when they first met.

'What was right for you wasn't necessarily right for me,' she flung at him. Were they having their first proper disagreement as friends? Why couldn't he see her point of view?

'But it's never right to please yourself and not consider its effect on other people, surely?' he argued. 'Especially when it's your family. Family is a bond that can never be broken or discarded like that.'

'I never intended to break or discard anything.' Melody's voice rose in annoyance. 'I just wanted to find my own way. What's wrong with that? Are you still accusing me of being selfish? I thought we'd got past that. I thought we were beginning to be friends.'

She stood abruptly, flaming in anger at him, and her chair fell over with a harsh crash.

'Do you always do everything for duty, Kieran? Do you never feel like just pleasing yourself?'

His eyes flashed dangerously and he stood too, close to her where she was immediately aware of his height over her.

'Maybe I will please myself,' he growled and pulled her to him, his lips hard upon hers.

She felt the thrill of it immediately and his mouth softened upon hers to a deep, searching kiss. His body was pressed against her and Melody moulded herself to him as their embrace tightened. Suddenly he drew away with a ragged breath, but she couldn't bear to be separated from him and placed her hands on the back of his neck to draw him in again, searching passionately with her lips against his in another searing kiss. He groaned, shifting her body to match his, as if he would never let her go.

The owl screeched close above them, its hunting cry shrill and shattering the air and they sprang apart as if suddenly jolted back to consciousness.

'I've got to go,' Melody mumbled.

She turned and half ran down the path to the cottage, never looking back once.

She slammed the door shut behind her and touched her fingers to her lips.

There was a small oval mirror on the living room wall, and in its reflection she saw a wide-eyed woman with full red lips and wild hair, looking utterly terrified.

She sank down onto the sofa, replaying what had happened. They had argued. Their views were very contrary. Then the kiss, which had been at once surprising and marvellous, but where did it leave them? What would she say to him when she saw him again and how would he react to her?

It complicated everything. She had intended to visit Barradale only briefly to sort out Skye's troubles before zooming home to Glasgow again to prepare for the upcoming fashion week. She couldn't afford to become entangled emotionally with someone — and on Barradale of all places!

It was only a kiss, she reasoned. It

was physical, it didn't have to mean that her emotions were involved. It could simply be a bit of harmless fun; after all, they were both grown-ups.

But she knew now from that kiss that what she felt was way beyond physical. Her heart and emotions were inextricably caught up in it too.

Against her better judgment, Melody realised she was falling in love with Kieran Matthews.

7

The door to the big house was wide open and Rona was playing in the hallway with an army of soft toys and battered-looking Barbie dolls. Beezer was sitting next to her, obediently wearing a red woolly hat and clearly part of the game.

'Hello, what are you up to?' Melody asked, arriving at the door. She was wearing her favourite salmon pink satin dress and a pair of her favourite shoes for courage. The taller the spike of heel, the more confident she usually felt. Today's were four inches but despite this, they weren't doing the trick and she had butterflies in her stomach.

Rona was oblivious to this and was busy arranging her teddies and dolls and one bedraggled giraffe into straight rows. 'It's school. I'm the teacher.'

'Is Beezer a pupil?'

Beezer looked at her with big brown eyes and a long-suffering expression. His tail thumped feebly.

'He's the top pupil,' Rona agreed. She bent Barbie's legs so that the doll sat forward on stiff straight legs, mature and out of place alongside the teddy and baby doll.

Melody felt out of place too. 'Is Uncle Kieran about?'

'No, he's gone.'

Gone? She had garnered all her nerve to come and see him in the morning, and he had to be here to listen! She had no idea what she was going to say, but she couldn't bear to stay away any longer after a long night tossing and turning, wondering what was going to happen between them next.

'Mummy's here. Would you like a cup of tea?' The childish voice was polite, echoing words of welcome she'd heard her mother say to visitors.

'That would be nice, Rona. Why don't I go and find her myself? I wouldn't want to interrupt your class.'

Rona nodded vaguely, having got absorbed now in providing each pupil with a small sheet of paper and a colouring crayon.

Melody found Elspeth in the kitchen, sitting with a cup of tea and a newspaper, propping her head on her hands and staring at the print. She got stiffly to her feet when she saw Melody, with no welcoming smile.

Melody's butterflies cartwheeled with abandon.

'If you're looking for Kieran, he's not here.'

'Rona just told me that.' Melody paused, uncertain. Elspeth didn't want her here. She should go. Most likely she blamed Melody for her brother taking off — and probably rightly so.

'I'd love a cuppa,' she said lightly, testing the waters further.

Elspeth nodded, still unsmiling, but poured her a large mug of brown tea from a chipped earthenware teapot.

'Where's he gone?' Melody tried again. She felt the reassuring slide of satin material as she sat down at the kitchen table in her favourite lucky dress. Luck that she needed right now to weather Elspeth's mood.

'He took the early ferry to the mainland. Claims he has business in Glasgow, but I don't know.' She stopped and stared at Melody sharply. 'What happened last night?'

Melody shifted in her seat with embarrassment. Could she really tell Elspeth about her passionate kiss with Kieran? Especially after the warnings she'd received from her.

'Sorry.' Elspeth sighed. 'That was rude of me. You don't need to answer that.' She looked away out of the window, which had a long view of trees and emerald hillside, before turning back to Melody with a weak but genuine smile, her eyes suspiciously shiny. 'I'm sorry, I'm still tired. It's none of my business what happened last night or why Kieran suddenly had a pressing engagement in the city today.'

'Stop apologising, Elspeth. It's understandable. You obviously have a strong desire to protect your brother. It's natural and very touching.'

Melody didn't add that it was also rather daunting for someone who wished to get a little closer to both Matthews. She hoped desperately that Elspeth wouldn't cry.

'Maybe it's not natural.' Elspeth shook her head, frowning into the lemon rays streaming through the kitchen window. 'Remember I told you how destitute I was when my husband died? I literally had nothing. No house, no job and no money. Kieran gave up his life in the South of France to save mine. That sounds very dramatic, I know, but that's the way it felt. It still does . . . ' She paused, her hand on her throat as if she could quell the rapid beat of her pulse. 'But the problem was that his wife, Sophie, also had to give up her life in France to come here to Barradale.'

'But she didn't take to it?' Melody guessed gently.

'That's an understatement. She was

112

livid! She wouldn't speak to me for the first three months when they moved back.'

'What? That's rather extreme, isn't it?'

'You've never met Sophie, so it's hard to explain. She was brought up to expect the best of everything. Her parents are incredibly wealthy and she was the only child. The impression I got was that whatever Sophie wanted, Sophie got. And that's not healthy for any child's personality or developing character, is it? She loved the whole Riviera lifestyle in Saint Tropez and I suppose it came as rather a shock to then be expected to live on a small, cold Scottish island.'

Melody guiltily found herself somewhat in sympathy with the absent Sophie. She too had found life on Barradale impossible after being forced to live there. Her only defence was that she had been a hormonal teenager and not a mature, married woman as Sophie had been.

'It's quite a lot to expect of someone, I suppose. To give up their whole life-style for their partner's family,' Melody replied rather cautiously.

Elspeth smiled wryly. 'And we paid for it big time.'

'What do you mean?'

'I knew we were asking a lot of Sophie, just like you say. Kieran knew it too, but he also thought that their marriage was rock solid and forever and of course he would have done the same for her, if things had been the other way round. He would have moved heaven and earth for the sake of her family without a second thought.'

Melody knew instinctively that her statement was true. Kieran's strong sense of duty to family would have meant he would have followed his wife wherever was needed to help out her relatives.

'But how exactly did you pay for it?' Melody prompted. She poured out two more mugs of tea for them.

Elspeth drank it gratefully, clearly

finding the whole conversation difficult, even painful. From the open door they could hear Rona instructing her class and the click click of Beezer's claws on the wooden floor of the hall.

'After the three months of silence were up, she moved on to bouts of anger and a lot of emotional manipulation aimed at Kieran. She eventually gave him an ultimatum — made him choose between her and me.'

'That's awful — and impossible.' Melody was horrified. 'That's not a choice anyone can make. He could hardly give up his own sister, and he couldn't give up his wife. It's crazy.'

'But Sophie was a little crazy then, you see. It was a horrible period for all of us.'

'Poor Kieran,' Melody murmured with genuine feeling.

Elspeth gave her a long stare and her face softened, as if Melody had passed a test.

'In the end Sophie left him. Kieran was a wreck. I sometimes wonder who he would have chosen if it came down to it. As it was, he was between a rock and a hard place.'

'What about you?'

'I was left with a mountain of guilt. It was my fault that Kieran's marriage disintegrated,' Elspeth replied with a heavy sigh. 'And yet, selfishly, I was glad he was here with me, to save me — and most of all for Rona. He gave her a place to live, food to eat and a secure future.'

Elspeth got up and paced around the kitchen, stacking plates and adjusting the onions in their Spanish ceramic bowl.

'The point I'm trying to make, in a very roundabout way, is that ever since then I've tried to protect Kieran from getting hurt like that again. He was devastated when Sophie left him and he hasn't really recovered from it yet.'

She came around the side of the table, leaving the dishes, and stopped in front of Melody. 'What I'm trying to say is that I won't stand in your way. I don't know what's going on between you and I don't want to, but I like you, Melody — and all I wish for is for Kieran to be happy.'

Now there were real tears welling in Elspeth's eyes. She rubbed them away with a shaking hand.

Melody grabbed her and hugged her hard and then they were both crying and laughing and hugging. Rona and Beezer came in to see what was going on and watched, puzzled, as the two women reaffirmed their fledgling friendship.

'The thing is,' Melody confided, when at last they had calmed down, 'I don't know if there *is* anything going on with Kieran. Perhaps we're just friends — which would be fine, too.' Now she was lying to herself.

'Whatever the situation, I'm glad you're here. I only wish you could stay longer.'

'So do I,' Melody said and was amazed to discover it was true. Barradale was no longer the enemy, the hated place it had been for so very long. It was weird how things could change topsy-turvy in the blink of an eye. Unsettling too, to have one's deeply held beliefs turned upside down. It made her wonder what else about herself was true and false.

'Do you want to stay for lunch?' Elspeth offered.

Melody looked at the clock in amazement. She'd been here longer than expected.

'No, thanks. I intended to go and see Skye this morning, although it's almost afternoon now. I'm still worried about her and I don't think I've helped her through her problems yet by any means. There's something eating away at her — something she's not saying.' Melody bit her bottom lip. 'Or it could be my imagination and she's just depressed and off-colour, although that would be enough in itself to be going on with.'

'If your visit doesn't help her, perhaps it may be time to get some medical advice.'

'You're right, but I really hope we can avoid that — it's too scary to contemplate.'

'Take some of this soup over to your mum's. It'll help if Skye's recovering from a tummy bug.'

Melody thanked her and got a hug from Rona and a waft of doggy smell from Beezer as she left the big house, feeling lighter and happier than on her arrival. She had Elspeth's support and friendship, which meant a lot to her. Not only that, but she now felt she understood more about Kieran from what Elspeth had told her.

She stopped dead in her tracks, half way down the path, as it struck her. Kieran had already had one woman in his life who had hated Barradale and it had turned out disastrously.

Why on earth would he want another?

8

The Harpers' house had a peculiarly long wedge of front garden exposed to the sea. During storms it wasn't unusual for clumps of seaweed to be flung up from the waves and tossed into the flowerbeds. Maeve Harper was weeding, a small bowed figure burrowing under the faded splendour of a hydrangea, its new season not yet begun.

Her face took on an anxious cast when she saw Melody, but she called out cheerfully enough to her daughter and laid down her trowel to meet her.

'Hi, Mum. How's the garden?' An innocuous subject and safe to talk about.

'Always demanding. There's couch grass under the shrubs. Goodness knows how it got there but it's a pernicious weed and the devil to get rid of.'

'Good exercise for you then,' Melody

joked, although her mother was so tiny and thin there was nothing to her at all. She hardly needed a workout.

'If you're looking for Skye, you're out of luck. She and Dad are away shopping in Gilfourth and won't be back until dinner time.' Gilfourth was a town on the other side of Barradale, large enough to boast a supermarket, a petrol station and a small public swimming pool. As these items were in short supply on the island, Gilfourth was a popular local destination.

'Oh. I'll come back tomorrow then, shall I?'

'Come in anyway. I'm about to have lunch. You can share my cheese and pickle sandwich.'

Melody found herself following her mother inside the house. Maeve's thin fair hair was ruffled from the wind and with a shock, Melody saw that it was now more grey than blonde.

How long had it been since she and her mother had been alone together? Possibly years, she realised. Probably going back to the dark teenage days on the island when she remembered with an unusual clarity Maeve sitting talking to her for hours in her tiny attic bedroom, trying to understand her tall, gawky elder daughter and trying to sort out all her angst and problems. Funny that the memory had resurfaced so clearly that she could almost see again her mother two decades younger, still pretty in a china-doll way, sitting on the delicate wicker chair in Melody's bedroom, her head cocked and listening intently to her daughter's many woes.

The detail of the memory was so vivid that Melody could visualise her own knees drawn up to her chest as she hugged them, perched on the single bed with its faded rose pattern coverlet. Maeve had hand-sewn the rose patches onto the cream material. It had taken her a week, and the colour and feel of the fabric had fascinated the young Melody so much that she had begged Maeve to show her how to use the old foot-treadle sewing machine.

She hadn't known then that it would grew into her passion and ultimately her career. It was strange the way things turned out and how slight, unremarkable actions could change a life's direction. Maeve had always been there in the background of Melody's life, taken for granted as a solid, never-changing part of her life. Yet, thinking of the sewing lessons and the memory of their soulful chats, Melody acknowledged she had had a quiet but huge influence on her life.

'Why didn't you tell me Skye was so unhappy?' Melody blurted out.

Maeve looked surprised. She let the fridge door swing slowly shut and placed the cheese and a jar of glistening green gherkins carefully on the worktop. 'I didn't want to worry you,' she said simply.

'But I had to find out from a stranger,' Melody said, aware of a note of petulance in her own voice. She thought of Kieran arriving on her doorstep, so cold and angry at her before he had even met her.

Maeve sighed. The kitchen tap let out a gurgle of water and she tightened it, letting the metalled water dribble away before answering, 'I knew if I told you, you'd be concerned and you'd come back to Barradale where you would be unhappy all over again. I thought your dad and I could cheer Skye up all by ourselves and you wouldn't ever have to hear about it.'

She sighed before going on. 'But Kieran persuaded us to let him bring you back. Skye started talking about you and insisting she needed to see you. So in the end your dad asked Kieran to please go and escort you home. I didn't want him to . . . '

'You didn't want him to? Even after Skye, Dad and Kieran had all agreed it was the best course of action?'

'No, I didn't,' Maeve said bluntly. 'You were happy and settled in your own world in Glasgow and I didn't want you taken away from that and brought back here. There was no need, or so I thought. But then Skye was so persistent I began to think I'd made a mistake, and in the end I was relieved when you returned. But I do want you to go back to Glasgow, to your life, as soon as you can.'

'You're protecting me from myself and I love you for it, Mum. But you know what? I'm beginning to think that coming back to Barradale has been good for me after all. It no longer holds any fear for me, the way it used to. I know I can come and go and not brood on it.'

'I'm so glad to hear you say that.' Maeve's smile lit up her face. She reached up both hands to cup Melody's face gently. 'I love you so much, you know.'

'I love you too, Mum. I only wish I hadn't been such a pest when I was younger.'

They both sat at the table as if their legs could no longer support them.

'Oh, you were a pest — but no more so than other teenagers,' Maeve acknowledged with a quick smile. 'And there were mitigating circumstances.'

She brought the cheese and the jar of pickles over to the table. Melody lifted the bread and knife and together they began to make their sandwiches for lunch.

'What neither you nor Skye know is the reason why we left Glasgow to live in Barradale. Maybe now it's time to tell you.'

Melody frowned, puzzled. 'But we know that already, Mum — we left because Skye was being bullied at school.'

Maeve shook her head and sliced a thin curl of yellow cheese onto the plate. She laid down the knife and looked directly at her daughter. 'Yes, that's partly why we left, but it's not the whole story. If it had just been the bullying we would probably have moved Skye to another school in the city. Goodness knows there were enough to choose from.'

'So what was the catalyst?'

'Your dad had a minor stroke.'

The bread knife fell from Melody's numb fingers.

Maeve nodded. 'It's true. If you remember he had a very stressful job as a warehouse manager. He was working long hours, unsocial hours and lots of overtime and we hardly saw him. After he had the stroke we decided that, along with Skye's school problems, it was time for a change, a downsize, so we shipped out to a more peaceful existence. Dad got the job here as shop manager in Marne's general store and that was that.'

It was as if a piece of puzzle had clicked into place to reveal a panorama in place of blocks of mysterious colour and shape. It explained why Maeve was always so concerned for her husband's health and why he was never allowed to lift anything and why everywhere he went he was offered a seat to rest and be still. Melody and Skye had bought into the whole 'looking after Dad' routine without ever quite knowing why.

Melody had a sudden fear. 'Could he

have another stroke?'

'It's very unlikely since he — or rather we — have made huge changes in our lifestyle to reduce the risks. So you see, Melody, the move to Barradale was positive for three out of four of us. We didn't realise you would react so badly to it, but in the end there was no choice for us, we had to do it regardless of your reaction. I'm so sorry, love. I was torn between your needs, Skye's and Dad's — and I'm afraid you drew the short straw.'

'Maybe if I'd known ... ' Melody trailed off. It wouldn't have made the slightest difference to her younger, angry self. She had been self-absorbed, the way kids that age usually are.

They ate the sandwiches, hardly tasting the food, both buzzing with all that had been said, shared and confessed.

Finally Maeve spoke again softly. 'I'm very proud of you, you know. You've carved out your own life, you're making a go of it.'

Kieran's words echoed in Melody's

head . . . *They talk a lot about you. Melody's done this, Melody's done that . . .*

She wondered what hopes and dreams Maeve herself had given up for her family. She had put their happiness first in their move to Barradale.

Family and duty. Why did Kieran's voice keep popping into her head? She was missing him; she loved him. The thought gave her a warm glow in her chest, like hugging a delicious secret.

'You may take after Aunt Rossy in looks but inside you're a lot like me,' Maeve commented.

'I used to think that I was adopted,' Melody confessed with a laugh. 'Until I met Aunt Rossy I was like the cuckoo in the nest — I looked so unlike you or Dad or Skye.'

'Oh, you're very like me,' Maeve insisted. 'Let me tell you why . . . do you remember how I met your dad?'

'At a music festival, wasn't it?' It was hard to imagine her little middle-aged mother at a festival. But Maeve was smiling warmly, looking inward into a fond past even while she sat in her gardening gilet, corduroy slacks and turtleneck sweater.

'Yes, that's right. I was only eighteen and I had just run away from home.'

'Run away from home? You never told me that part before!'

'I didn't want to give you similar ideas. I wasn't happy at home so I packed up and left one night. I was going to go back someday, I suppose, but then I met your father and that was that.' She shrugged.

'We travelled around, took jobs here and there and lived a rather bohemian lifestyle,' she went on. 'When you eventually turned up we became more conventional and settled down in a way that, ten years earlier, I couldn't have contemplated. We've been lucky — we've had our ups and downs but we've always been happy in each other and in our children.'

Melody was reeling from this new information. She knew her parents had married young and her grandparents had disapproved, which was why they didn't see much of them, but she had no idea her mother had been such a rebel!

Melody's grandparents lived on an isolated farm in the north of Scotland. She'd only met them a handful of times as a child, and had been intimidated by their dourness and their sombre house. No wonder her mother had fled, if that's what her home had been like!

'It was very wrong of me not to go back,' Maeve was saying. 'I've made my peace with my parents now, of course, but it leaves a bitterness on both sides when things are left unresolved for too long.'

She laid her hand over Melody's. 'I'm telling you this because I was terrified for a long time that history was repeating itself. You ran from Barradale at twenty, but yet you kept in touch so I'm thankful for that. You're back now for a little while and I know it's cost you emotionally, but it's also a chance

131

for me to finally explain all this and get it off my conscience.'

'You don't need to feel responsible for my behaviour back then,' Melody told her. 'And I do feel better about Barradale now, as I said. I'm glad you've told me all this, but I'll need a bit of time to digest it.'

'And nowhere better to mull things over than in the garden,' Maeve announced cheerfully. She looked like a woman whose burden had lightened. Her confessions to Melody had released a tension she'd carried inside for so long and she was more relaxed, her shoulders back and her head held higher. 'Come on and help me weed the last patch.'

Melody knew nothing about gardening except that it would ruin her clothes and shoes. Maeve persuaded her into a pair of wellies, Dad's being the only ones that would fit her feet. She also lent her a waxed jacket to cover her dress. She led the way out to the breezy front garden and showed Melody the plantains which had chosen the wrong bit of ground in which to grow.

'They need to be pulled up by the root or they'll spring up again.' Maeve demonstrated on one unfortunate weed, twisting until the earth broke, revealing white worm-like roots.

'Kieran came by this morning on his way to the ferry,' Maeve added casually.

Even hearing his name spoken was a sweet pleasure. Oh, she certainly had it bad! Melody dug hard at a weed. 'What for?'

'To see how Skye is. He's very thoughtful of her, isn't he?'

'He's that kind of person,' Melody agreed. The weed clung on, battered but resilient in the soil.

'I wondered if there was something more to it than just kindness,' Maeve said mildly.

'I shouldn't think so. There's a ten-year gap between them.'

'There's ten years between me and your father. No, I just wondered if you'd noticed anything. He's a lovely

133

young man, I'd be delighted if he and Skye liked each other that way.'

Melody stabbed at her chosen weed more viciously. Kieran and Skye? Impossible! Besides he wouldn't have kissed her so thoroughly if he was interested in her sister. He was too honest a man for that, she would swear to it.

'I'm sure he sees Skye as a younger sister, that's all. He's worried about her but he's not romantically involved, I'm certain of that.' The plantain finally gave up the battle and let itself be ripped from the flowerbed and flung with more energy than strictly necessary onto the heap of garden waste.

Maeve slid a glance at Melody and gave a little secret smile which her daughter missed. 'It would be good for Skye to meet someone nice. It might make all the difference to her recovery.'

'I'm sure you're right but I don't think Kieran's the man for her. There are plenty of other men on the island.'

'Oh well, that's true. Gosh, look at

the size of this tap root. What a horror!'

They worked on together companionably. There was a lot of satisfaction to be had in beating up the soil, Melody discovered. It was hard work and therapeutic — if a little hard on satin. She found herself enjoying the time outside with her mother now that the air had been cleared between them. She had new facts to paint a better picture of her family and how they fitted together.

* * *

John and Skye Harper returned exhausted in time for dinner and were delighted to find Melody visiting. She stayed for a meal and observing Skye subtly, felt there was some improvement in her mood — though she would at various points feel Skye's eyes upon her and somehow knew that she still had more to say.

* * *

Melody reached the cottage late. Dusk had descended and the first few pipistrelle bats were flitting and darting in the air, hunting for moths and midges, as neat in their movements as tiny birds.

There were two messages on her mobile when she switched it on. She'd turned it off during dinner, wanting only time with her family uninterrupted by the outside world. The first message was from Harry.

'Hi sweetie, just a reminder we're coming to see you on Saturday. Come and join us for dinner at the hotel on Saturday evening, okay? There'll be me, Niall, Sara, Catherine and whats-her-name, the assistant . . . Jade, is it? Oh, and if you can finish those designs you promised me, I'd be sooo grateful. Byee.'

What on earth was Catherine Sommerlee doing coming to Barradale? She'd been so derogatory about island life that Melody would have bet good money she would never set foot on an island in her life. It was very odd.

And the designs — Melody could see a late night looming. She hadn't even started on any sketches and Harry wanted the finished product by the weekend!

Her mind was blank of creativity and she decided on a small glass of wine to help stimulate ideas, then remembered the second message.

It was Kieran. He started hesitantly, almost formally, 'Melody, I hope you can hear this. The line is bad,' She could hear him over the crackle, his voice like melting butter on hot toast.

She shivered with longing for him and listened as he went on, 'I'm sorry I couldn't see you today but I had work to do here. Anyway, I'm hoping you might agree to join me for dinner on Saturday night. I've a few more meetings here in Glasgow, but I'll be home on the Saturday morning ferry and I'll hope to see you then.'

Yes, yes, yes — she'd love to go to dinner with him on Saturday night!

Then it hit her. Saturday night she was also now invited out with Harry and the gang. Blast it. What should she do?

9

Melody stood shivering on the harbour looking out across a pewter sea to the miniature ferry which was growing larger with every minute. She was wearing her woollen trousers with a cerise blouse under her thick sheep's wool lined leather coat and she was still frozen. The pain and encroaching numbness of her toes reminded her of the stupidity of bringing only thin strappy sandals and party shoes for a Scottish island break.

To add to her misery, she had a splitting headache and was absolutely convinced she looked terrible. She blamed Harry. In order to get her latest set of designs completed she had worked constantly the last few days and then late into every evening.

Every night when she finally stopped, she would peer into the bathroom mirror as she brushed her teeth and see how white her face was and how red-rimmed her eyes.

This morning she had slapped on an extra layer of foundation and generous helpings of liquid mascara to mask how much she had been neglecting herself.

Although she usually worked alone and preferred it that way, this time she had been joined by a curious Rona and Beezer on the second day. Rona was content to sit silently with Melody's fabric scrapbook and paper to draw while Beezer took the opportunity for another well-earned sleep. They appeared the following days, too. Melody found herself anticipating their arrival and was strangely comforted by their presence as she worked.

She was nervous at meeting Kieran again so she paced up and down, upsetting the seagulls which were standing on the harbour edge, beady eyes ready for any dropped food. They laughed raucously at her and flew about her in circles. The smell of oil was making her nauseous, and off the harbour edge there was a slick of it, a thick glutinous rainbow sliding on the surface of the black water in time with the motion in her stomach.

'They'll be here in another five minutes,' Skye shouted to her over the noise of the birds, the slap of the water on the wood and the car engines idling as drivers queued to get the ferry to the mainland.

It was a crazy place, Melody decided, and about to get crazier with the arrival of Harry and the gang off the ferry. Skye was jumping up and down trying to keep warm. She was well wrapped in a cotton puff jacket, jeans and boots and a blue bobble hat, but she didn't have an ounce of spare flesh to insulate her. Still she was grinning excitedly and Melody found herself grinning back in spite of her mixed feelings at greeting the ferry.

She was glad she'd asked Skye to join her and it seemed only fair since she hadn't spent as much time with her sister as she'd hoped to so far. She was desperate to see Kieran; it had become a physical ache, but she had no idea how he would react to her. Was it too much to hope that he had fallen in love with her too, or was it just a casual attraction for him?

'Here it comes,' Skye yelled as the ferry horn blasted out with a great shudder that reverberated in their chests. Then there was a thump as its side smacked into the harbour wall and men raced to rope it and put up the gangplank shipshape.

A stream of people flowed across to solid ground. Who would have imagined so many people wanting to visit Barradale, Melody mused inconsequentially.

And then there he was; his tall, broad-shouldered figure stood out in the crowd. He was smartly dressed in a suit, holding a briefcase and overcoat, his black hair tamed but his blue eyes as dark as ever, searching the clusters of people until he saw them and waved.

Melody's heart danced while Skye was still jumping and waving madly. He strode confidently from the gangway and made his way over to them, his gaze fixed on Melody's. What should she do? Her immediate impulse was to kiss him and hug him as if he belonged truly to her — but he didn't, did he? She half raised her arms as he reached them. He dropped his briefcase at his feet, his gaze steady.

Then a sudden loud scream had them all turning in distraction. It was Sara, leaning over the gangplank railing, waving frantically to Melody and screaming, 'There she is! Melody! Melody, we're here!'

Melody dropped her arms, Kieran picked up his briefcase, Skye stuffed her hands deep into her pockets and they all watched as the gang approached.

'She's beautiful,' breathed Skye in awe.

Catherine Sommerlee was drifting regally out of the queue off the ferry, looking every inch the snow queen. Her white hair shone in the weak sunshine and her dark eyes were lidded, giving nothing away.

'Her hair's just like Fiona's,' Skye said.

Melody remembered then how pale Fiona's hair had been. The only difference was that she had worn it short and cropped close to her head, whereas Catherine wore hers long and flowing to maximum dramatic effect.

'Don't worry,' Skye said in answer to Melody's unuttered question, 'I'm fine talking about Fiona, really. I'm practising each day letting her go. I know I can do it. Having you here is making me stronger and Kieran's right — Fiona wouldn't want me to be sad forever. She was always so upbeat herself, she'd have hated for me to be miserable. She'd scold me awfully.'

This last was said with a tremor in Skye's voice. There were limits, after all, to what could be achieved on a daily basis. Melody hugged her. There was no need for words — and no time either as

Harry arrived with them.

'Darling! So good to see you. What a terrible journey.' He kissed Melody theatrically on both cheeks and stood back to admire Skye. 'Oh, do introduce me!'

Then Sara was there hugging her and complaining about the choppy crossing, while Catherine let Niall carry her two large bags towards them.

Melody hurriedly introduced everyone, conscious of Kieran beside her and hoping he wouldn't choose to slip away in the mayhem. But he appeared to be in no hurry to leave Melody's side and cordially shook hands with them all, seemingly quite at ease, even with strangers from the city.

Catherine flicked back a sheet of shining platinum hair over her shoulder as she met Kieran. For once she was smiling and her hand lingered in his until he disengaged her grasp to be introduced to Jade, who was flushed and panting, having run off the boat to catch up.

'Are you all right, Jade?' Catherine asked sweetly.

Jade twitched nervously. 'Yes, I'm fine, thank you.' She looked ready to chew on her nails.

'I only ask because you look a bit hot and sweaty and I was worried you were ill. It's too cold to sweat, surely?' Catherine wrapped her white cashmere coat more snugly round her where it emphasized her long elegant body — which was the idea.

'Come on, I think we should hurry along to the hotel in case Jade is unwell,' Catherine said, sounding tritely concerned and grimacing as a clod of mud attached itself to the toe of her pale suede boot.

'I'm not ill,' Jade protested feebly, but Catherine had an iron grip on her shoulder and she let herself be led by her caring employer out of the grubbiness of the harbour and up to where the hire car was waiting.

At the car Catherine turned with a stiff smile to Melody. 'Lovely to see you. Dinner at eight?' Her smile thawed as she included Kieran in her gaze. 'Will you join us?'

Melody was annoyed with herself, with Catherine and Harry and with the whole situation. There had been no opportunity for her to speak to Kieran alone and explain the problem with dinner tonight and the double invitation. Now Catherine Sommerlee was lording it over them all as if they were under a spell. It was Harry's job to take control of the gang, yet he had apparently relinquished this role to Catherine without so much as a squeak.

'You're very kind, I'd love to,' Kieran said smoothly. 'In return, once you've all unpacked and refreshed yourselves, why don't you join us for lunch?'

He gave a set of directions to Harry for Aucher while Melody stood stunned beside him. This most definitely wasn't in the plan for the weekend. It was a disaster waiting to happen.

Niall packed the bags into the car boot and they all bundled in with Harry at the wheel. He wound down the driver's side window and winked at Melody. 'See you later, darling,' he called, and the car revved and accelerated off at far too fast a speed for the sleepy harbour road.

They were left with the stench of exhaust fumes and a sudden peaceful silence. The ferry had gone again, taking the pedestrians and the car queue with it. Kieran's car sat alone in the car park ahead.

'It was kind of you to invite them all for lunch,' Melody said uncertainly.

'They're your friends. I'd like the chance to get to know them,' Kieran said.

'I didn't get invited to dinner,' Skye added indignantly.

'Come anyway.' Melody felt bone tired and her head was thumping. 'It's going to be a crowded event.'

Bitterly she imagined a romantic candlelit dinner for two, just her and Kieran. Although a moment later the cautious voice in her head reminded her that yes, he had suggested dinner, but he hadn't hinted at romance. Was it a date or not?

Melody felt like crying because now she would never know.

'I'm sorry I didn't get a chance to tell you about Harry's dinner invitation,' she said to Kieran.

'Not a problem. I'm looking forward to dinner tonight. I love a crowded event,' he teased, quirking an eyebrow at her as he expertly drove them up the road and along the way to Aucher.

★ ★ ★

Elspeth had taken the news of five extra lunch guests in her stride and Melody helped her make soup and freshly baked rolls, while Skye and Kieran tidied the dining room and set the dining table for a meal.

They had barely simmered the soup and disposed of three stacks of paperwork from the room before there was the hoot of a car horn and the noise and chatter of people at the front door. Rona ran to let them in.

'This was such a good idea of Harry's,' Sara giggled to Melody after lunch as they walked arm in arm in the woodland. It was still a cold day but somehow the temperature had lifted, enveloped by the trees, with the breeze halted through the branches and the soft leaf litter under their feet.

'I admit I was a bit surprised when he said you were coming to visit,' Melody said cautiously. 'I didn't think it was your scene — any of you.'

'Catherine put him up to it, actually.'

'Catherine?'

'Yeah. She didn't actually come out and suggest it but she dropped hints left, right and centre until Harry got the idea and thought it was his own.' Sara laughed out loud.

'Why would she want to come to Barradale?' Melody was completely baffled.

Sara's tone dropped to a confidential hush and she glanced around. There was nothing to be fearful of as Catherine Sommerlee was beyond them by some distance talking to Kieran, her pale head bent close to his dark one to pick up on what he was saying.

Something primitive flared in Melody's chest but she pushed it down and listened to what Sara had to say.

'She's got a thing about you.'

'What on earth do you mean?'

'You're, like . . . the competition. Remember you told her that, the night of Harry's party?'

'Yes, but it was a joke. I'm not really competing with her, or I don't mean to be. Besides, her designs are quite different from mine.' But that was not the case at all. Melody remembered the pictures in the magazines of Catherine's work so similar to hers, the images flashing through her mind.

'She didn't take it as a joke,' Sara went on. 'She's ruthless when it comes to work. I've seen a few altercations between her and people she works with and it's not pretty. She's agreed to give

Niall and me some dresses to sell in our boutique but it's all on her terms. She can be quite nasty if you oppose her.'

It was on the tip of Melody's tongue to comment that Niall didn't appear to mind, but she held it back. Sara probably didn't need Niall's worship of Catherine pointed out, however one-sided it was.

'Why deal with her and socialise with her, then?'

'She's good at what she does. It makes good business sense to stock her dresses and bandy her name about. Women love her stuff, she's new and exciting.' Sara quickly touched Melody's arm. 'I don't mean your stuff isn't — you know your dresses sell like hot cakes and you've hardly time to fill the orders for individual wedding dresses. Which is why Catherine wants to find out all about you. She's determined to win.'

Melody flung a stick into a rubbery-leaved rhododendron, startling a flock of chaffinches. They rose, chirping, to land high in a Scots pine, safe from further surprises.

'That's plain silly. There's nothing to win.'

Sara looked meaningfully ahead to where Catherine was still keeping pace with Kieran.

'Isn't there?'

★ ★ ★

Harry burst into the forest clearing with Rona chasing him. He kicked the football high and ran to get it, allowing Rona to nip in front of him and reach it first.

'She's too nifty on her feet,' he moaned, pretending to collapse on the ground, making Rona laugh gleefully. The freezing surface had him leaping up again fast and the football game went on, with Rona winning by a whisker each time. She was loving the attention.

'This reminds me of growing up on the farm,' Sara said, clapping enthusiastically as Rona caught the ball, hugged it to her and ran, dodging Harry's inept attempts to catch her.

'You grew up on a farm? You never told me that,' Melody said, astounded. 'I thought you were Glasgow born and bred.'

'I am,' Sara said. 'But we lived on a farm on the edge of Glasgow until I was six, then Dad sold up and we moved to the city centre.'

Catherine had moved, unnoticed, beside her and shuddered delicately. 'I wouldn't admit to that if I were you, Sara. It's nothing to be proud of.'

Sara flushed and became suddenly flustered. 'No, no, you're right, Catherine. I was just saying to Melody . . . '

'Farms and islands . . . honestly, between the two of you it's country bumpkins all the way,' Catherine sneered.

Melody noted how Catherine picked her moments. Kieran was on the other side of the clearing with Harry and Rona, playing ball, and she got the feeling it didn't matter to Catherine what anyone else thought.

154

Sara was subdued. The fun had left her face. It made Melody mad that she would let Catherine treat her that way. There were other ways to keep the boutique afloat. There had to be.

Harry came up, handsome and ruddy from the exercise, his blond hair sticking up on end, which in no way detracted from his good looks.

'She's a great kid,' he puffed. 'But I'm worn out. Told you Harry Gordon turning thirty was a terrible idea.'

'Rona's a fantastic footballer. She tricked you by not 'fessing up to it.' Kieran arrived and tousled his niece's hair.

Rona was delighted with all the attention and clearly besotted with her new friend Harry. It wasn't often she could persuade her mum or uncle to play ball as they were always so busy.

'Melody, you look frozen.' There was concern in Kieran's voice as he assessed her. 'I can't help with a pair of proper shoes but you can take my jacket.' Before she could protest, he had draped his jacket around her shoulders. His lips twitched at the sight of her unsuitable footwear and she wrinkled her nose at him as if a secret message had passed wonderfully between them. She was sure he was remembering his disapproval of her Blahnik green sandals when they first met, and her unsuitable outfit for cycling.

His jacket was warm from his body heat and smelt deliciously of him. She felt she could stay in it forever.

'Kieran . . . you promised to show me the badger sett?' Catherine's dark eyes slid subtly between them.

'Of course, it's over there inside the woods,' Kieran said politely. He tucked his hands into his jeans pockets and led the way, sauntering relaxed and casual along the no doubt familiar woodland path and into the shadows of the trees.

Catherine flicked a glance over her shoulder at Melody and a tiny triumphant smile momentarily snaked across her lips.

'No man ever turns her down, you

know,' Jade said glumly.

'There's a first time for everything,' Melody replied quickly. She didn't want to think about it. Was Catherine's power really so great?

'I'm just warning you, that's all. Don't be surprised if she turns his head. Men love her, she's a magnet to them.'

'Kieran isn't . . . ' Isn't what? Melody settled for saying, 'We're not dating anyway.' It sounded lame.

'But you'd like to be. It's okay, you don't need to deny it. It's pretty obvious you like him and he likes you. But that won't put Catherine off. In fact she loves a challenge, so it'll just make her even more determined to have him.'

Melody took a good look at Jade. She saw a rather self-conscious, plump girl with unfashionable freckled skin and frizzy ginger hair. The baby pink sports fleece was a style disaster, made worse by being mismatched with khaki cargo pants and thick-tongued black rubber trainers.

She was simply 'Catherine's assistant' — Harry had even, carelessly cruel, called her 'what's-her-name' — and none of them ever saw her in focus. And yet Jade had cleverly sussed out Melody's feelings for Kieran in a nutshell — in fact the whole situation, at a glance.

Jade shifted uncomfortably and nibbled a flange of skin around her forefinger, knuckles curled, white and nubby.

'Sorry,' she mumbled, 'That was out of turn.'

'No, no.' Melody shook her head.

'I know what you're going to ask. Why am I working for Catherine if I dislike her so much?'

It wasn't what Melody was going to ask. She wasn't intending to prolong the conversation at all. She was uneasy at what both Sara and Jade had revealed about Catherine and uneasy, too, at the length of time it was taking to locate a badger sett. At least Kieran and Catherine wouldn't be alone. Harry, Sara and Niall had wandered along the path as well, with Rona skipping ahead.

'Thing is, my mum knows Catherine. They went to school together back in the day,' Jade continued, oblivious to Melody's stray thoughts. 'She wangled the job for me. I was desperate to get off the island and start a real life so I went for it. Let's face it, there weren't any jobs at home anyway. But I hate it and I hate her, she's so mean to me and I hate fashion and design.'

Now Melody was listening.

'What would you like to be doing instead, then?'

'I want to work with horses — that's my dream. Nothing fancy like being a show jumper or a jockey, just mucking out the stables and looking after them, curry combing and braiding their manes for shows.' Jade's young face lit up as she spoke and she looked suddenly pretty with her enthusiasm.

You could never tell with people what was going on inside, Melody decided. She would, until recently, have described herself as a good judge of character, but since coming back to Barradale she was doubting her ability.

Her picture of people she knew was askew. Her mother, Skye, Sara and even Jade were telling her things about themselves and their world that she had never even suspected. Her tiny mum confessing to running away from home to live life as a hippy. Skye's reaction to Melody's teenage anger, Sara's revelation about growing up on a farm and now Jade's secret passion for horses and a life far away from fashion.

It was all making her head spin.

* * *

All in all, Melody decided that lunch had been surprisingly successful. The gang appeared to have enjoyed themselves so far on Barradale, Kieran and Elspeth had been wonderful hosts and everything had run smoothly.

Even her headache had gone and she felt, overall, much better. So it was with a light heart and a sense of anticipation that she later dressed for dinner at the hotel. She chose her favourite green sandals first and matched them with a lime and olive skirt and a cream silk blouse. She fastened an unusual verdigris pendant on a copper chain around her neck, brushed her hair until it shone and checked her make-up.

She felt great — and what's more, she knew she looked great too! She grinned at the girl in the mirror and stuck her tongue out. It was time to have fun.

If she had known then how the evening would turn out, she would've locked the cottage door and refused to budge outside.

'You look really lovely,' Kieran said softly when he arrived to pick her up, his eyes shining as he looked at her.

'You're looking pretty good yourself,' Melody said, linking her arm into his proffered one. He was wearing a cobalt blue shirt that matched his eyes and a pair of charcoal trousers — smart but casual. They walked to the car like a couple, easy in each others' company but with a physical awareness that rippled under the surface.

'What's that?' Kieran indicated the long, thin case Melody was holding.

'It's some designs I owe Harry,' she explained. 'He always gets first viewing of my new wedding dress creations and I value his comments on them. Then when I'm ready he gets to photograph the finished dresses for the magazines. Perfect system . . . ' She hesitated, the images of recent magazine shots flashing in her mind. She still needed to speak to Harry about that, to put her mind at rest.

'Everything okay?' Kieran asked, opening the passenger door for her and acknowledging the taxi driver with a friendly nod.

'Yes, fine.' It was probably nothing but coincidence. She relaxed into the plush of the seat. She'd think about it later.

The gang had already bagged their

table and two carafes of wine were already flowing. Their buzz of chat and laughter was louder than anywhere else in the room and more than the sedate Barradale Hotel was used to. Two couples dining at the far end of the room looked over, frowning a little.

It was a reasonably large dining room with an elaborate glass chandelier centrepiece and glass uplighters casting a soft yellow light over the tables. The table linen was crisp and snowy white, and each table was completed by a unique posy of hot-house flowers and a glass candlestick. The flickering flames of the candles lent an intimacy to the room. The waiters glided from table to table bringing full plates and menus.

'Here they are, the happy couple,' Harry called, raising his wine glass to them.

Melody cringed at his words but Kieran squeezed her fingers gently in silent reassurance as they took their seats.

Catherine's face was thunder for the

briefest of moments at Harry's remark before she hid it in a blandly welcoming smile.

If anything she was more beautiful than ever, Melody thought unhappily. She had dressed for the occasion, except that her idea of smart but casual was a thin scarlet woollen dress that clung to her model curves, leaving little to the imagination. She had teamed it with slim leather boots on impossibly slender heels and her trademark white hair flowed like molten silver down her back. What man could resist her?

Jade's words came back to haunt Melody. Why had Kieran taken the empty place next to her? Melody slid into the seat between Kieran and the end of the table where Skye was sitting, looking relieved to see her.

The conversation during dinner was light and amusing and Melody relaxed into it, enjoying her peppered steak and salad and a glass of good red wine. The carafe at her end of the table lasted well, while Harry was ordering more at an alarming rate at the other end.

As they ordered desserts Kieran stood and excused himself. His mobile phone, while on silent, had vibrated a business call and he had to take it outside.

Catherine nodded in a proprietary manner but Kieran's apology was to Melody.

She smiled at him. 'Hurry back,' she said, and meant it.

Harry was getting louder as the night wore on and in this mood even Niall wasn't capable of taming him. She watched Kieran's strong back as he went outside and felt somehow less without him.

She turned back to feel Catherine's black gaze upon her. Harry was chatting up the waitress again and the girl was giggling — until the hotel manager nodded her away with a reproving jerk of the head.

'More wine, we need more wine!' Harry said in a terrible imitation of a Barradale island accent.

'Harry, please keep it down a little,'

Melody whispered.

He waggled his fingers at her in a disapproving sort of way. 'Oooh, look at you! You've gone all island girl on us, telling me to be quiet. You'd never do that in a Glasgow nightclub, darling. You need to get home before you go completely native.'

Harry laughed uproariously at his own comments and slopped wine as he tried to refill his glass.

'You have to admit, Melody, it is all a bit Hicksville.' Catherine leaned over Kieran's empty seat and spoke conspiratorially. 'You must be so relieved you moved to the city. So many opportunities for you to better yourself.' She was practically purring.

'Actually, Catherine, I'm pleased to be home. Returning to Barradale has been like a blast of fresh air to me and I feel revitalised.' Melody spoke calmly and clearly.

At the end of the table Harry spluttered while Sara's jaw dropped. Jade gave a little thumbs-up, unfortunately caught by Catherine whose glare suggested there would be retribution for such rebellion later. Quickly Jade snagged a fingernail and began to chew.

Skye was kicking Melody under the table, either to stop or to continue or to run away, she didn't know which. All she knew was that a surge of anger was washing in like the highest wave on the crest of the sea. All at once her worlds were colliding and she was torn between them.

She had so looked forward to dinner and finding herself amongst her friends and familiarity, but when she looked afresh at them she saw superficial, vain and snobbish veneers. Was she like that, too? Was that what Kieran had seen when he first looked at her — and did he see her that way still?

Yet they had their good qualities, too. Sara was her best friend, for goodness' sake. She'd admitted her enjoyment of the day out at Aucher and evoked memories of her country childhood. Harry, for all his flirtations and roguishness, had played ball with Rona, so kindly letting her win. And Niall was just Niall, never with any real bad side to him.

She was torn between loving them and hating them — and between her city life and defending Barradale. Melody's headache was back with a vengence.

Catherine looked ready to move in for the kill, but before she could make her move, there was a resounding crash as Harry fell drunkenly, taking his chair with him, legs in the air. It would have been hilarious if Melody had been in the mood for laughter.

Waiting staff rushed forward and the table erupted with people moving and loud voices as they went to help Harry. Only Catherine sat, unmoved, as calm and icy as the snow queen in her blood-red dress.

Between them Kieran and Niall managed to half lift, half drag a bleary-eyed Harry up the stairs and into his hotel room.

'Is he okay?' Melody asked anxiously

as Kieran arrived back at the waiting taxi. Skye hunched forward in the back seat to hear.

'He'll have a sore head in the morning but other than that, he'll be fine,' Kieran reassured them.

They travelled in silence to drop Skye off at Marne, enveloped in the wrap of velvet darkness with the sea glittering with orange sparkles from the house lights.

Catherine's parting words hammered in Melody's head. She had taken the opportunity to speak to Melody while Harry was being put to bed.

Melody turned to Kieran as the taxi left them, its rear tail lights winking like the devil's eyes.

'I have to return to Glasgow tomorrow,' she told him.

'Then I'll come with you,' he said quietly.

He leaned forward and kissed her briefly, then turned and merged with the night on his way up to the big house.

Melody touched her burning lips, then she hurried inside to pack her things.

10

A hysterical Leila Doves had begged Catherine to finish her wedding dress. She was sure that Melody wouldn't be back in time before her dream wedding and Catherine, of course, was only to pleased to help.

Melody opened her front door and felt herself relax. She was home. Leila's dress was still centre stage in the living room and, assessing it quickly, Melody knew she could finish it in no time at all.

She dropped her bags, flung off her coat and began adjustments, humming as she worked. Kieran was staying at a hotel in the city centre and had accepted her invitation to dinner at her flat this evening. Little darts of excitement and nervousness twinged in her stomach at the thought of it — an evening of just her and Kieran, together in the intimacy of her small dining room.

She was busy patching together a menu in her mind when Leila arrived. She almost ran to Melody, gave her a big hug and blew her nose noisily. She had been crying.

'Oh, Melody, I can't believe you're back! You've no idea how horrible it's been waiting for you and wondering if you'd ever return. I've had the most ghastly migraines thinking about my poor dress, wilting on its stand, only half done. And then Sam and I had the most awful fight . . . '

Here she shook her head vigorously and smeared her mascara with the back of her hand, 'But it's back on now, so you do need to finish it — you must!'

The wedding dress was hardly wilting on its mannequin, nor was it only half done. In fact, with a huge sense of relief Melody realised it was almost ready. She still wasn't one hundred percent pleased with the line of the bodice and she would have to take up the hem of the skirt by a few millimetres to adjust for the ivory silk shoes that Leila had chosen.

But suddenly she was desperate to be done with it — and with Leila and her on-off fiancé Sam.

'You know, Leila, it wasn't very nice of you to ask Catherine Sommerlee to finish it for you.' Melody kept her tone mild, despite her re-emerging annoyance at it. 'I did tell you that I'd be back in time. You know I wouldn't have let you down.'

'Oh, gosh — no, I didn't do that! How could you think it of me?' Leila's big, wet eyes were round and innocent. 'No, what happened was I was in Manchester at a wedding show — I needed to get my wedding favours and I decided on the most gorgeous little velvet pouches, each with five almonds . . . ' she paused to press her splayed hand to her chest, remembering presumably how lovely the favours were.

'And you were there with Catherine?' Melody prompted.

'No, no. She introduced herself and gave me her business card,' she explained. 'It was so wonderful meeting her, especially as she had a collection of dresses on display. I couldn't believe it when she spoke to me. She even helped me pick my favours — how fantastic was that? — and she told me she knew you were designing my wedding dress, but that you probably wouldn't get back in time to finish it. I almost died when she said that!'

Melody handed Leila a tissue and carefully steered her away from the delicate ivory silk of the wedding dress. Make-up stains would be a disaster at this stage.

'But then she marvellously offered to do it herself to help both of us out. She said you would want her to help me . . . ' she chewed her lip. 'Was it wrong?'

'No Leila, it's fine.' Melody didn't want her client hyperventilating so she kept a lid on her anger. 'It's all worked out. Your dress is ready and if you can wait just a bit, I'll press it and wrap it for you to take away now.'

Now Leila really burst into tears; tears of happiness, she assured Melody once a pot of tea had been offered and accepted.

Leila sipped her tea noisily as Melody finished the last minute rituals of preparing the dress. She prayed hard that Leila and Sam would make it through the next few days at least until the ring was on the bride's finger, the ink had dried on the registry book and the wedding dress had been worn and admired.

Once she had waved a final goodbye to Leila, Melody picked up the telephone and made a few calls.

They confirmed her worst fears.

★   ★   ★

Dinner preparation was going downhill fast like a dolly cart on a rollercoaster. Melody had managed to set the table and get dressed in time, but somehow the cooking was far more difficult than the step-by-step pictures in her cookbook would have her believe.

Melody was not a natural cook and ate more ready meals than she ought to. But lemon chicken with wild rice and sautéed greens sounded delicious — and easy. Except she'd forgotten to marinade the chicken three hours earlier and the wild rice was burning and sticking. She tried desperately to waft away the acrid black smoke as the rice welded itself in a crispy layer to the bottom of the pan.

The doorbell rang.

Kieran stood there looking effortlessly gorgeous and Melody's heart did its familiar little flutter as he stepped past her into the house.

'Need some help?' Kieran asked, his lips twitching in amusement at the fug emerging from the kitchen at the back and spreading nicely into the living room.

'It's more like a miracle that I need,' Melody yelped.

Kieran handed her a bunch of perfect white roses, shrugged off his jacket and went in search of the source of the smell.

When she joined him, having put the beautiful roses in a vase in the living room, his sleeves were rolled up and he was manfully tackling the rice pan and the uncooked chicken.

'Lemon chicken?' he asked, one eyebrow cocked at the cookbook on the counter top.

'With wild rice and greens — except I forgot to pre-prepare the chicken and I've burnt the rice and I've no idea how one sautées beans.'

Kieran grinned. 'Well, it's the thought that counts.'

'Yes, but I'd love to eat it, too,' Melody said glumly.

'Not to worry — Elspeth's taught me a thing or two about home cooking and Sophie was a great cook too, actually.'

Sophie. His mysterious, awful ex-wife. Melody couldn't even compete with her over culinary skills, as she had none!

But it was the first time Kieran had mentioned Sophie and Melody was careful, not wanting to reveal Elspeth's confessions.

'Sophie was your wife?'

'Ex-wife. It was a long time ago . . . ' He sliced the chicken expertly and slid lemon slices into the oven dish.

Melody took her place beside him at the worktop and tried to top and tail the beans. Her shoulder brushed his and a tingle ran through her body. Kieran grinned at her and she was flooded by not only desire but happiness. He was here, beside her, in her home and they had the whole evening ahead of them without distraction or interruption. His dark blue eyes sparkled as he watched her feeble attempts to trim the green beans.

'Let me show you,' he said and stood behind her so that his hands could rest on hers.

'There is an actual chopping technique that chefs use,' he explained patiently, folding his fingers around hers and over the heft of the knife.

But Melody was no longer interested in the greens as she felt the lean length of him against her back, his breath wafting her hair, the feel of his skin on hers where their hands touched. She let the knife go and twisted in his arms to face him, hungry for his lips and his caress.

'Melody,' he whispered and their lips met in a searching kiss, deep and powerful, leaving them both wanting more. Kieran drew away for a brief moment, then groaned and drew her to him again for a longer kiss, as if he would take the very core of her with his caress.

Finally, Melody pushed him gently from her.

'Hey, dinner's going to burn again,' she joked feebly.

He trailed a finger across her cheekbone, leaving a tingling trail, then briskly moved the food to the oven and onto the hob, not speaking but concentrating on the task.

What was he thinking? His blue eyes

were solemn when she caught his gaze and her heart sank. Was he remembering Sophie? Was he still so in love with his ex-wife that he regretted kissing Melody? They were suddenly awkward with one another and whereas Melody had anticipated an evening of intimacy alone with him, now she felt the minutes elongate.

'Is everything all right?' she asked finally as they sat at the dining table with two steaming plates of lemon chicken.

'Of course,' he said stiffly. It was as if their bodies had never entwined with passion just minutes before. 'I got the feeling something was bothering you when I arrived?'

It was safe territory and a good change of subject. If Kieran didn't want to discuss their attraction for one another, then so be it. So Melody told him of her suspicions regarding Catherine Sommerlee. How she had tried to steal Leila Doves away, and a few other potential clients. Some of those that Melody had phoned were downright cagey where a few weeks before, they had been keen to get her to design and make their dresses.

'Couldn't they just have changed their minds?' Kieran asked. 'It's an emotional time for people, getting married.'

'It's not just that, though.' Melody sighed. 'I can't prove it, but I think she's stealing my design ideas too.' She got up and fetched the wedding magazines to explain.

Kieran frowned at the images. 'How would she have got hold of them?'

'That's the worst part,' Melody said solemnly. 'I think Harry might be passing them on to her.'

There, she'd said it. It was too awful to contemplate that one of her best friends could do this to her, but there was no other way Catherine could be getting them.

'You'd have to be very certain before you accuse him of that.' Kieran sounded serious.

Melody nodded miserably. 'I can't bear to ask him. I keep hyping myself up to speak to him and then not doing it. What if he confessed? What would I do then?'

She pushed the lemon chicken around on her plate, her appetite gone. There was no answer to it and she didn't expect Kieran to provide one, but it felt good telling someone about her fears. She could hardly discuss it with Sara or Niall.

She realised with a jolt how much she'd come to depend on Kieran's company in the short time since they'd met.

'Enough about my problems,' she said, trying to change the mood. 'Tell me about you, and about Sophie.'

His face darkened and she mentally kicked herself for letting Sophie slip into the conversation. Of course he felt badly about her — Elspeth had made it plain he adored her.

Then he masked his expression and smiled bleakly. 'As I said it was a long time ago. Ancient history. She left me because of Barradale and I don't blame her.'

'You don't blame her leaving you

because you moved to be with your family?' Melody said incredulously. 'What kind of love is that?'

'It came as a shock to Sophie. We were living in the South of France and we had a sophisticated lifestyle and then suddenly I needed to return to Barradale for Elspeth's sake. It was too much to expect of Sophie.'

'But love — real love — doesn't depend on where you live,' Melody persisted. 'It's eternal, it's all-encompassing.'

'I don't believe that,' Kieran said flatly. He pushed his plate away. 'I think love is a combination of factors, including time and place. Think about it, you may meet someone and fall in love with them in your teens or twenties, but you both know you're too young to settle down and so it can't last. Or you meet someone, fall for them, but they're about to leave the country for another job, say. It would have to be a very special bond to overcome distance.'

'But if you truly loved each other, then one of you would sacrifice their job and home to move country and be together.'

'It doesn't work that way in real life.' Kieran shook his head. 'I've known couples in these situations. Most of the time they split under the pressure. Successful love affairs and marriages are those where both people are at the same time of readiness for love and who want to live in the same place.'

Was he still talking about himself and Sophie, Melody wondered — or was he trying to give her a message? That they may share a bodily attraction but there was no future in it because he lived in Barradale and had no intention of ever leaving it, and she couldn't live there, rooted as she was in the city? *He's never said he loves you*, Melody reminded herself. *There's a spark for sure, and we've shared kisses and embraces, but that's all.*

She changed the subject, steering it onto safer topics, such as books they had read and their musical tastes, but his words rang in her ears and she had to work hard to smile and laugh and keep up a pretence of enjoying the evening.

It had soured. But what had she expected from him — a declaration of undying love? They hardly really knew each other. It was her own fault for falling in love with him so deeply and so irrevocably that she could never reverse it. And Melody knew in her heart, even if Kieran didn't, that time and place and convenience had nothing to do with true love. She would have followed him anywhere if he asked. Even to Barradale.

They did kiss again at the end of the evening when Kieran left for his hotel, but it was a chaste and friendly kiss on her cheek. If Melody had looked carefully from under her thick fall of hair she would have seen his troubled eyes, but she didn't.

She waved him out and sat on the sofa amongst the CDs they'd picked out, next to the drained espresso cups and the remains of the New York cheesecake (bought not baked), and she knew what she had to do.

She had to return to Barradale one more time and find out once and for all what Skye was hiding. Only then could she get back to work and prevent Catherine from destroying her client list and reputation. If Skye still needed help, Melody determined that she would bring her little sister back to Glasgow and get medical support if required.

As for Kieran Matthews, she had not a single idea. Was he interested in her or not? And what would happen when she came back to Glasgow for good? Would she ever see him again?

* * *

It had taken all of Keiran's willpower not to take things further that evening. But maybe that was what he needed to do to get Melody Harper out of his mind . . . an affair between two adults who both knew the score?

Kieran slammed his hand down on the hotel dressing table and winced at the pain. If only it would bring him to his senses.

The trouble was that he knew instinctively that an affair with Melody would not be enough. She had got under his skin emotionally and the more he spent time with her, the deeper he was falling. The guard around his heart was fracturing because of one tall, flame-haired woman with wide hazel eyes and kissably full, soft lips.

He wanted to protect her from harm — her stories about Catherine and Harry had alarmed him on her behalf. But most of all he enjoyed her company, her conversation and just being with her. He hadn't felt this way about anyone since Sophie.

Kieran stopped pacing his hotel room abruptly. Could he be falling in love with Melody? That would be a catastrophe; it would be history repeating itself.

He visualised her in her inappropriate shoes and scant summer dresses, shivering in the harsh Barradale wind. She was out of her natural habitat on the island; she was a hothouse flower, a city girl and she needed the props of civilisation — just as Sophie had. It would never work.

Kieran opened his laptop ready to work, but his head was full of Melody . . . the scent of her light flowery perfume, the way her hair curled behind her ears, her dark lashes against her pale, flawless skin.

He *was* in love with her! But instead of giving in to his newly realised feelings, Kieran pushed them down viciously. Had he not told her that love depended on the right time and place? Well, the timing was terrible and would never improve — he would never get involved in a love affair ever again if it meant going through what he had gone through with Sophie.

As for place, Melody had made it very clear what she felt about Barradale. It was impossible. The best thing he could do, he decided, was to stay away from her until these feelings had simmered down.

The phone rang and he picked up.

'Kieran, it's Melody.' A tinny pause on the line with the faint echoes of other voices — ghosts in the machine or a crossed wire somewhere. 'Just to let you know that I'm finished here and I'm going back to Barradale to see Skye. Are you going back tomorrow, too?'

There was a thinly disguised longing in her voice and he suddenly realised that she felt it too — this need to be together. It would be so easy to go back with her, but he felled the idea brutally short.

'No, I won't be. I have work to do here and I'll probably be a few days at least. Perhaps you could let Elspeth know when you see her?'

By the time he went back to Barradale, Melody would have returned to Glasgow for good and they need never cross paths again. It felt like torture, like pulling out a tooth, but it was for the best for both of them. It was madness to prolong their attraction, he knew that now.

'Okay, yes, I'll tell Elspeth.' He could hear the disppointment in her voice and it twisted in his heart. 'Kieran . . . ? No, never mind . . . goodbye then.'

Click.

The receiver went down at the other end with a note of finality.

Kieran swallowed hard. He released the phone and shoved it away as if it were the enemy. He had got what he wanted. Melody was out of his life, or soon would be. He knew it was the right decision.

So why did he feel so desperately and utterly miserable?

11

Melody stood doubtfully in her brand new hillwalking boots. They were clumpy and heavy on her feet, and they combined with thick green woollen hillwalking socks to give her an alien sensation at the end of her toes. Her feet were used to better!

'Do I look like you?' she asked Skye.

Skye hunkered across from her, struggling to squash the last of their provisions into a blue canvas rucksack. She was wearing similar boots, except that hers were bashed and old with some cuts and abrasions to the leather. She was warmly dressed in a waterproof jacket and under-layer of fleece, with waterproof trousers over stretch running leggings.

'Yep,' she confirmed. She rammed a red woolly hat down over her fair hair, reminding Melody of Beezer's head-gear.

'Great. And we're doing this again why?'

'Because it's fun. And because you look like you need cheering up. And because we need to talk, and this way we'll be sure of total privacy.' Skye grinned.

I look as if I need cheering up? Wasn't it meant to be the other way round? Melody thought wryly. Skye was the one who was meant to be feeling low in spirits and Melody was meant to be helping her, not wallowing in her own misery.

At least it looked as though Skye was finally ready to talk honestly and openly about whatever was bothering her. Then Melody could hopefully go home and forget Barradale and forget Kieran Matthews once and for all. As if that was possible.

'Are you worried about climbing the hill? You shouldn't be. Fiona taught me how to map-read and use a compass. I never wanted to learn to climb with ropes and gear like her, but I did enjoy walking in the hills. We had some laughs,' Skye said, tightening the strap on the rucksack, although it was secure enough. She smiled sadly at Melody.

'I'm not worried,' Melody reassured her. 'I didn't realise you and Fiona went hillwalking,' she added gently.

Skye nodded. 'Some of my best memories of Fiona are with a backdrop of blue sky and grass. She loved the outdoors.'

'This is good, Skye. It's good to talk about her.'

'I feel better all the time. Everyone says you must see a year through after a bereavement but I just needed longer.'

But there was still something on her mind — it was obvious to Melody — there was a haunted look in her sister's eyes. She hoped fervently that Skye would tell her today what else was bothering her.

Elspeth came out of the back door of the big house to watch them. They were leaving for the hills from the Aucher Estate where the path through the woodland led steadily upwards to the distant peaks.

'I've forgotten my first aid kit,' Skye exclaimed suddenly. 'It's in the car. I'll be back in a moment.'

They watched her walk round the side of the house, her head tall and her step jaunty.

'She's so much better,' Elspeth remarked. 'It's all thanks to you, Melody, for agreeing to come back and see her.'

'I don't think I can take all the credit,' Melody answered. 'Time is a great healer. Her recovery was on its way even before I arrived. But whatever the reason, I'm very glad. She seems so much happier and we're closer as sisters now.'

'How are you?' Elspeth stared closely at her. 'You don't look happy. I guess my brother has something to do with it. Is that why he hasn't come home?'

'I don't know what's going on. It's my own fault. I've fallen in love with him but I don't know how he feels about me.'

Elspeth hugged her. 'If he's got any sense at all, he'll fall in love with you, too. Just don't expect it fast; he had a terrible time after Sophie left, but he's ready to move on, even if he doesn't know it yet.'

'I'm not sure he is.' Melody took a deep breath. 'What if he's still in love with Sophie?'

'Then he's a fool,' Elspeth said smartly. 'He needs to wake up and see what's in front of him. You'll be good for him — and for me. I'll enjoy having a sister-in-law I get along with.'

'That's confidence,' Melody said, her voice a little wobbly. She didn't share Elspeth's conviction that Kieran knew what he was missing. He was positively trying to avoid her by not coming back on the same ferry.

'It'll be all right, Melody, trust me. Be patient with him and don't give up on him, please.'

Skye joined them then with the first aid kit and there was no time to speak further. Rona came out to wave goodbye and the two sisters set off along the track still rimed with morning frost glittering in the bright day.

The path soon led into the wood-lands, reminding Melody of Harry and the others. They would all have returned to Glasgow by now. She'd texted them when she left so suddenly for the city and wondered if Catherine had realised why she'd gone so promptly. Was Harry regretting his behaviour at the hotel? At some point she was going to have to confront him. But not now.

Now, she promised herself, she would immerse herself in the day and focus on Skye, who still needed her.

Their feet crunched on fresh leaves of wild garlic, releasing its pungent odour into the air. Melody could hear the creak of her new boots where the leather stretched and gave and softened. Chaffinches trilled to each other high above, and the air was fresh and crisp and inviting.

'I could get used to all this outdoor lark,' she called to Skye, who was marching steadily ahead of her.

'I hope you'll still be saying that when we reach the summit.' Skye pointed to the dark peaks which looked very far away and unnervingly high.

'How long will it take us?'

'Four hours there and back. It's not far.'

Not far! It sounded far to Melody. Still, perhaps if she pounded her feet long enough up and down the hill, she could forget a certain pair of dark blue eyes, an Irish lilt and strong arms pressed around her. And his kisses. A bolt of longing for him pierced her with physical pain. *Stop thinking about him. Focus on the steps. One, two. One, two. Creak, creak, creak.*

After a while, the path left the woods and started to climb more steeply, weaving its way between rocks and tussocks of brown rushes and up past a lonely lochan of peaty water where a single wagtail flicked its tail at them as they plodded by.

Melody's heart was thumping against her bones, threatening to break free,

196

and her breath came in gasps. She was unfit. She spent her days sitting sketching and sewing, or standing pinning and draping. She didn't stride about on a regular basis. Now she wished she did.

'Can we stop?' she puffed at Skye, who still looked fresh and relaxed. Only high colour in her cheeks gave away that she'd walked steadily for an hour.

Skye glanced at her watch. 'It's time for a break anyway. Fancy a chocolate bar and some juice?'

They found a large flat-topped boulder to perch on, overlooking the lochan. At the base of the boulder, in the bare mud to the water, were the delicate paw prints of a fox. It was a whole different world up here, where animals and plants lived their lives unseen by people. Melody was aware of the vast volume of open space stretching for miles around them. A sense of peace stole over her.

'If I snapped my fingers, I'd vanish in an instant,' Skye said, bringing Melody firmly back to earth.

'What does that mean? What are you talking about?'

'It's silly but I keep thinking it. How temporary all this is. It looks solid and everlasting but it's not. Fiona went out one day and didn't come back. It could happen to me or you or anyone.'

'Yes, but it's unlikely. It'd be terribly bad luck if it did.'

'But it could happen, that's my point.' Skye turned to her. 'In fact it did happen, to Fiona. That's why I needed you to come home. I realised I had to tell someone in case I don't ever get the chance to.'

'Tell someone what?' Here it was. The reason Skye had asked for her. Melody's heart rate had settled to normal and the chocolate and orange had topped up her blood sugar level nicely, so she was calm and ready to hear whatever it was that Skye had to tell her.

'You remember the day you, me and Kieran went cycling and we talked about Mum and Dad and our move to Barradale?'

Melody remembered it in fine detail. She had known then that Skye was not fully unburdened.

'We moved to Barradale because I was being bullied at school,' Skye went on. She plucked little tufts of moss free from the boulder and threw them. One landed on the water and bobbed away.

'Yes, I know all that,' Melody said patiently.

'But you were so unhappy and it spoilt everything. I know now why Mum and Dad never got angry at you throwing your bike in the sea. They felt guilty at making you leave Glasgow. But it wasn't their fault. It was mine!' Tears were streaming freely down her cheeks and she made no effort to mop them up.

'No.' She shook her head when Melody would have touched her. 'No. When you hear what I've got to say, you'll hate me.'

'I'll never hate you Skye. That's impossible.'

More moss was torn up and flung down. Then Skye's hands were clutched together in her lap.

'I was never bullied at school.'

'Yes, you were. It's why we left.'

'I lied. I was unhappy at school. I was bored and then I had a fight with my friends and I wanted to change school so I told Mum and Dad that I was being bullied. I never imagined for one minute we'd leave the mainland. I thought I'd go to another school in Glasgow. It just snowballed and I couldn't say anything. I'm so sorry, Melody, I'm so sorry! I messed up your life and then I was too scared to admit what I'd done.'

'You've lived with that all these years?' Melody whispered.

'It's got heavier and heavier. Then Fiona died and I knew I had to tell you before it was too late.'

Melody reached out for her little sister and Skye let her pull her into a warm and loving embrace. 'You should have told me.'

'I couldn't. You were always so angry about it and Mum and Dad were concerned about you and me and I didn't want to add to their problems.'

'They weren't concerned so much for us,' Melody told her. 'And you mustn't take all the blame to yourself. You see, Dad was sick and they wanted to move away from Glasgow anyway.' Melody told Skye what their mother had told her about their dad's stroke and the need for change.

'Why didn't they tell me?' Skye was horrified.

'Probably for the same reasons you couldn't say what you had done. As a family we've been far too good at hiding our emotions, and that's got to change.'

'Can you forgive me?'

'There's nothing to forgive, Skye. I'm only glad you've finally told me and got it out of your system. I love you, you're my only sister and nothing can change that,' Melody said, her throat caught with emotion.

Skye's eyes had lost their haunted expression and were shining with tears and relief as she murmured, 'I want us to be so much closer. Can we do that?'

'You can start by visiting me when I get back to Glasgow. Come and sample the big city highlights.' Melody laughed.

'What about Dad?' Skye asked. 'Is he okay really?'

'I think so. But between us we can keep an eye on him and Mum. They're not getting any younger and it's up to us to look after them now, isn't it?'

Melody reached out her hand to help Skye up and together they stood on top of the large boulder looking out at the wonderful world. Below in the valley, Aucher looked tiny, the big house like a doll's house surrounded by knitted trees and patchwork fields. As they looked, a dark shadow passed over the valley. Skye glanced up ahead in the direction they would take to the hills.

'Looks as if the weather's closing in. We should get going.'

'Isn't the forecast for a dry, bright day?'

'Maybe the clouds are coming in

quicker than predicted,' Skye suggested, shrugging. She lifted her rucksack and slung it over her shoulders before jumping down to the ground.

Melody stretched her legs. She could feel the muscles crying out. She put on her own rucksack over aching shoulder blades and stared at the still distant peaks. There were black clouds hovering over them and a muzziness that suggested it was raining on the summits.

She jumped down beside Skye who grinned uncertainly as if to check they were still okay with one another. And they were. Melody had been shocked by Skye's revelation, but not angry. They had both been young and foolish. It was time to forgive and forget and to move on together. So she smiled back at her sister with genuine warmth, and Skye's gait took on confidence as she led the way onward to the hills.

They had only gone a further ten minutes when the heavens opened and cold icy rain lashed down on them.

Melody pulled up the hood of her jacket and stumbled on, feeling the chilly drops leak down her neck and under the collar of her borrowed fleece, making her shiver.

There was a sudden piercing cry. Skye was sprawled in the wet marsh, her rucksack hitting her head as she went down. Her left leg was at an awkward angle and Melody saw she had stepped in a hidden, water-filled ditch. She ran forward and gently slid her hands under Skye's armpits. She was heavy because of the lump of trapped rucksack, but carefully and slowly she pulled her away from the ditch and helped her to sit up. Skye moaned. Her face was white and had a clammy sheen.

'I think I've broken my ankle,' she whispered shakily.

Melody peeled back Skye's trouser leg and rolled down her woollen sock. Where her skin met the rim of her boot, it was purple and puffy and darkening as they watched.

'We need to get help fast,' Melody said. She fumbled in her rucksack for her mobile phone and switched it on. There was no signal.

'Blow the whistle,' Skye said faintly. The bright orange rescue whistle was tucked in the top pocket of the rucksack. Melody knew she had to blow it six times, short and sharp blasts. Skye had told her that, this morning back at the house.

Aucher and Elspeth, comfort and safety seemed all of a sudden so very far away. A harsh wind had risen up, blustery and squally and, with rising panic, Melody saw that visibility was fading as a miasma of damp mist encircled them.

She blew hard and shrill on the whistle, but the sound vanished into the mist. She frantically pulled stuff out of her rucksack. There was an extra fleece which she wrapped round Skye and a scarf which she tucked round her sister's neck. Should you feed a casualty or not? Melody couldn't remember. In fact, had she ever known the answer? She took a calculated risk and decided it was better for Skye to be warm and she had a vague notion that sweet, hot tea was good for shock.

With cold, trembling fingers she wrestled the lid off the aluminium flask and poured the steaming liquid. Skye drank it gratefully, her lips thin with pain.

'You have to leave me here and go and get help,' she said.

'I'm not leaving you — you're hurt!'

'You have to. It might be hours before someone hears the whistle. No one's going to be out in this weather now.'

There was logic in what she was saying, and Melody reluctantly agreed. 'Okay, but let me wrap you up first. There's one more fleece in your bag. I'll leave you the food, the flask and the whistle.'

She sorted the stuff out and tried to create shelter out of the rucksacks to protect Skye against the wind and the rain.

'I'll be back as soon as I can with help,' Melody promised. She hoped Skye couldn't see her fear.

She walked back down the path they had struggled up and disappeared into the mist. The rain turned steadily into sleet — and then into snow.

*　　*　　*

Melody could hardly see her boots in front of her. She had long since given up on looking ahead and now concentrated on the brown leather uppers which contrasted darkly with the snow. But the slush and sleet had turned to fat feathery snowflakes which clung to her clothes, her feet and even her eyelashes, making it almost impossible to see anything. The world had closed down to a few white centimetres and only muffled sound.

She could hear her own breathing inside her ears, raspy and uneven with exertion and fear. Her woolly hat and jacket hood pressed down on her head, keeping her vitally warm but limiting her senses yet further. Despite her fleece layers and good quality jacket, she could feel icy air seep in to her body. She checked the zip and poppers with increasingly stiff and painful fingers. The coat fasteners were shut, so why did she feel so cold? She wished again that she'd remembered to bring gloves.

She hoped Skye was surviving up there alone on the hill. It was the knowledge that she had to get help for her sister that drove her forward and kept down the anxiety and the dread that otherwise threatened to burst out. She had to keep her nerve.

The problem was that this situation was totally unlike any she had been in before. She was well out of her comfort zone. She might as well have been on the surface of the moon for all she knew what to do.

Come on Melody, be brave. You can do this, she told herself sternly. *One foot in front of the other. One steadying breath after another. Ignore the chill in your body.*

It was hard to believe it was the same day. They had set out in bright sunshine for a relaxing walk and had finished in a nightmare. Skye had told her that weather conditions could change very quickly in the Scottish hills but she hadn't listened, not really. It was such a lovely day, it hadn't seemed relevant. Except that now it was and Melody was out of her depth.

She was exhausted so she sat for a moment in the snow. The white flakes swirled around her and the wind howled.

'I'll rest for just a minute,' she said out loud. It felt better to hear a voice, even if only her own. 'Then I'll walk faster. I'll get help soon, Skye, I promise.' Something loomed in front of her.

'Who is it? Can you help me?'

A frightened bleat answered and a soggy bundle of yellowed wool trotted by. It was a sheep caught out in the storm.

'Poor thing, you're scared like me.' It was starting to seem normal, talking to herself. 'Right, I need to move on. It's so difficult to make myself get up. I could just stay here and rest.'

With a struggle, Melody stood and peered in despair at the ground. She was following a small river track, no bigger than a trickling burn. A while earlier she'd somehow lost the path. Logic told her that the burn she'd then found must run down off the hills to low ground. So if she simply followed the river track she would get back to civilization and help.

But she couldn't see it any more. Blindly she knelt, scooping out soft handfuls of granulated snow in front of her to find the track. It wasn't there — she'd lost it!

'It doesn't matter. I just keep going down,' she told herself and stumbled on. After a while she realised in alarm that she was going up. It was so disorientating in the storm that she was actually retracing her steps. She turned again, but now was totally lost. She had no idea where she was or even whether she was going up or down. Not only that, she felt funny. Her head was light and she could see black spots dancing in front of her eyes and her tummy was nauseous. She had left Skye all the food and drink. How long was it since she'd last eaten?

'I wish I'd told you that I love you,' Melody said loudly. Kieran couldn't hear her but she needed to say what was in her heart. 'I'm in love with you and I always will be.' She wiped her face with a numb hand. 'I wish you were with me. I could do with your strength right now.'

Thinking of Kieran gave her an unexpected surge of energy. Perhaps it was the knowledge that she might not survive the storm, might never see him again. Or perhaps just loving him warmed her blood. Whatever it was, Melody was able to walk on through the void, hoping desperately she was descending.

Ahead of her a patch of darker nothing appeared.

'Hello! Hello! I need help!' She half ran towards it, her clumsy boots banging excruciatingly against the back of her ankles. It was a house — or at least a shack. She ran her hands over it, feeling rough brick and then the splintered wood of an old door. She pulled it open and fell inside. The wind screamed and flurries of snowflakes blew in after her. Melody struggled to push shut the door and bolt it.

All of a sudden the air was blessedly still. Melody peeled off her sodden hat and shook out her hair. What was this place? It was sparse. She was in a bare room with brick walls and a dirty wooden floor. A lopsided, battered table was propped up against the wall under a single, grimy window. There was a large fireplace in the room but it was empty of coals. There was nothing else except a second door. Melody went through the door to discover only another similar bare, inhospitable room. She went

212

back to the first one and sat down near the fireplace. There was no food, no water and nothing to cover herself with. But at least she was out of the storm. She was shivering badly and an agonising tingle began in her fingertips as they thawed.

'Should I stay here?' Melody asked herself. Her voice echoed strangely in the empty room, bouncing off the exposed brick of the walls. 'I need to get help, but I also need to have energy to do that.'

She decided to wait out the storm for an hour before continuing on. She reasoned that this gave her enough time to warm up her fingers. If only she could set a fire, she could dry off her coat and hat and socks. Maybe in an hour the storm would have abated. She'd be all the faster going down. Skye had food and drink and layers of clothing to keep her insulated so an hour would be okay . . . she hoped.

Melody's teeth chattered uncontrollably and the porcelain clink of them annoyed her. There was a peculiar buzzing in her ears too. The black spots still danced merrily in front of her eyes. She hated that they were so happy when she was not. How dare they sing and dance when she felt so sick? Didn't they know that Skye was in danger? The storm was around her, viscous as syrup. Skye was in the eye of the storm.

Suddenly Melody knew she couldn't linger. She had to save Skye. She crawled to the door and passed out.

12

She was in a dream, a wonderful dream. She was cosy and warm and she floated in the centre of a giant orange ball. The ball bounced lazily up and down but she didn't feel sick any more; instead the motion was soothing like a baby being rocked in its cradle. There was even a lullaby being hummed over the cradle of the orange ball. If she listened closely, she could almost pick out the words to the song.

As her senses returned and her world sharpened Melody honed in to the comforting buzz. It was a voice, a man's voice, repeating the same thing over and over again.

'Come back, Melody. Come back, sweetheart. I love you.'

She half opened her eyes in confusion. Kieran was holding her, rocking her and murmuring over her with no idea that she had heard him. She shut her eyes again.

The orange ball was in reality the glow from a crackling fire in the hearth which sent out a surprising amount of heat into the bare room. She savoured the fact that she was warm and safe, held in Kieran's arms.

I love you. Had he really said that, or was she still in a dream within a dream? He was still murmuring to her. She felt his lips on her forehead in a tender kiss and the roughness of his workworn fingertips as they gently smoothed her hair away from her face. She could lie here forever, not asking how or why Kieran was here. She would marvel only that her wish had been granted and he was here now, exactly when she needed him most.

She risked half opening her eyes again to glance at his familiar handsome features.

'Melody — you're awake! Thank God.' He raised her with the strength of his arm until she sat, still cradled

216

against his chest. She could feel his heartbeat and the solid mass of him, all lean muscle and quiet power.

In astonishment she saw that she was no longer wearing her hill walking jacket or jogging trousers, nor her hideous ugly boots and woolly socks. Instead she had dry clean cotton trousers, furred over-boots and a thin lilac fleece. She blushed. Kieran must have undressed her while she slept and then clad her in these new clothes, probably borrowed from Elspeth.

'Here, drink this. No, don't talk yet. Drink first.'

She obeyed and drank the hot soup gratefully. Then as she finally felt the world click into place, her first thought slammed like a hammer against her skull.

'Skye? I have to get to her! She's dying out there!'

Kieran kept her in his grip easily. She stopped struggling and look at him questioningly.

'It's okay,' Kieran soothed. 'Skye's in good hands.'

Melody slumped in relief and didn't notice how naturally she curled into Kieran's arms.

'What happened? How do you know she's fine?'

'When you didn't return on time Elspeth raised the alarm. Some of the estate workers are good mountaineers and they set off to find you. They found Skye first,' he explained. 'You saved her, Melody — she was still core warm because you'd piled all those layers of clothing onto her and had given her all your provisions. Making a small shelter out of the rucksacks was a good idea, too. For a city girl, you did marvellously well.' He squeezed his arms round her, his tone teasing.

Melody leaned in to him, glorying in his closeness. Her senses were no longer dulled, but now hyper-sensitive to his body heat, his touch and his masculine scent.

'Where is she now? Is her ankle going to be okay?'

'The guys took her down the hill and

straight to the island hospital. Her ankle's broken as she suspected, but she was very stoical and brave when they had to move her. She's going to be fine,' he assured her.

A spark burst noisily from the fire onto the floor. Kieran swept it back into the grate with the end of a cut branch.

'How did you get here?' Melody asked curiously. 'You were in Glasgow . . . '

Kieran looked sheepish, 'Actually no, I wasn't in Glasgow. I was already on the way home when Elspeth phoned to say you were missing.'

'But you said you were staying in Glasgow another few days.'

'I changed my mind.' He flung another log on the fire causing it to spit furiously.

'You should have set a fire as soon as you found this place.'

'There was no coal or sticks,' she protested.

'There's a whole cupboard of them.'

Kieran helped Melody to stand gingerly on weak legs. She grabbed his arm for support. It was a good excuse to touch him.

Kieran led her through to the second room and pointed. There at the far end in the corner was a dun-coloured door she hadn't noticed in her cold, spaced-out state.

'There's firelighters, matches, the works,' he grinned.

'Why would anyone leave all that stuff anyway?' Melody snapped. 'It's a stupid waste storing it in an old shack where no one ever goes!' Neatly ignoring the fact that she had gone there and had she seen the cupboard, could have been warm and snug and possibly avoided fainting.

Kieran laughed. It was a rich, happy sound which ricocheted off the walls. 'It's not an old shack. Well it is, but we prefer to call it a mountain bothy. It used to be a shepherd's cottage but now it's a shelter for those that need it.'

'Oh.' That took the wind out of her sails until she saw the funny side and gave a snort of laughter. That set her off further and then they were both laughing and Melody didn't know why but it felt good, as if she were releasing all the terror of being alone and frozen in an alien landscape.

'Luckily I got to you before you had completely welded to the ground in ice,' Kieran said, sobering up.

'How did you know where to look for me?'

'I came up the hill with Tam and Geoff, our estate workers and we found Skye first. We couldn't get much sense out of her; she was confused and possibly delirious, but I got the gist of it that you'd gone back down to get help. So I left Tam to organise getting Skye downhill to the medics and I followed your trail.

'It wasn't easy because more snow had fallen on top of it and it wound round itself like a crazy snail trail. I reckoned you'd make for the bothy if you saw it, so I came here in the hope you had, and found you out for the count.' Kieran cleared his throat.

'For one horrible moment I thought you were dead.'

'For a while I thought I might not survive the storm,' Melody admitted. She remembered shouting out her love for Kieran at that moment of realisation.

'People do die in the hills in Scotland . . . ' Kieran said.

'We were well equipped,' Melody argued. 'Skye knew how to use the map and the compass, she's done the route several times, she told me.'

'What about you? Could you use the map and compass? Were you familiar with the route? Do you know first aid?'

Melody felt a flare of anger. He was treating her like a silly child. She was a grown woman and quite capable of making her own decisions. She didn't need Kieran to take care of her. All this must have shown on her face because he sighed.

'I'm not getting at you, Melody, I want you to be safe. You're not used to the hills or to outdoor activities.'

So there it was. That barrier between them, that gaping crevasse. Kieran was on one side in Barradale and she was on the other in Glasgow.

Why had he returned from Glasgow early anyway? She realised he had neatly sidestepped having to answer that very question earlier by wrong-footing her. Well, he wouldn't get a chance to do that this time.

'Why did you come back early? You didn't answer me.'

He stuck his hands in his pockets, his black brows drawn down, his hair wind-tousled and wild. He kicked at the embers of the fire. Outside it was pitch black and the wind howled like a banshee.

'I don't know,' he said finally. He ran his fingers distractedly through his hair. 'I swore to myself that I wouldn't see you again. That it was the best thing for both of us.'

Melody winced — was it visible? Had he seen it?

'At your house,' he went on, 'it was a

madness, kissing you and wanting you. I couldn't see a happy ending to it for either of us. So I knew I had to keep away.'

It hurt to hear him say it. Was it so awful sharing kisses with her? Was it so bad that he had to run away? He could see no happy ending for them, and yet, he was here. She had heard him say he loved her — hadn't she? She was suddenly unsure. Perhaps it had been part of her dream after all.

'But you did come back,' she prompted.

'I couldn't stay away from you,' he said and his dark blue eyes met hers. 'Even if it is madness, I can't control it.'

'You said you love me . . . ' Melody whispered.

'You heard that? I thought you were still asleep.'

'If you'd known I was awake, would you have told me?'

'Yes. No. I don't know . . . ' Kieran looked exhausted. There were lines grooved from his nose to the sides of his mouth from weariness, and with a guilty twinge she realised it had been a long and arduous day for him, too.

'Come on, we're both tired, let's sit down in front of the fire,' Melody suggested.

'Are you sure?'

Of course she was sure. She was drained of strength despite the fire and the soup, but when they sat together she clicked as to why he'd asked — his very proximity was heating her up like a fire. He had taken off his jacket and was wearing a tee-shirt that moulded itself to his muscled torso and accentuated his powerful shoulders and broad back. His long legs stretched out beside her, almost burning where they touched hers.

She held out her hand for his and clung to it like a lifeline. He was here, and that was all that mattered now. His instinct had been to come to her. He loved her.

'I love you,' she whispered to him.

'Are you sure?' he asked again,

seeking out her gaze.

Melody felt a flicker of excitement.

The old bothy was more welcoming in the low light of the fire. Angles turned to blurred shadows and the pane of glass in the single window reflected back the flames. It was as if they were the only two people alive, and it felt good and right.

Melody leaned into Kieran and kissed him. With a sigh of desire he pressed his mouth down on hers, his hands on her waist under her fleece.

'I love you too,' he said huskily as he kissed her.

The fire roared beside them as they lay down on the blankets Kieran had brought. They had the whole night ahead of them in the intimacy of the bothy, surrounded by the fierce elements and protected by brick and tile.

Melody shivered happily. Kieran, mistaking it for chill, drew her in closer, moulding his body to hers so that she could feel the heat of his desire for her, while the light from the bothy flickered like a tiny beacon high up on the louring hillside.

★　★　★

Melody woke early next morning. A shaft of pure sunlight streamed in through the dirty glass onto her face. She scrunched up her eyes. The fire was out, the coal and logs reduced to a pile of dove-grey ashes. She smelt soot and smoke and dust. It was cold without the flames.

She hurried to dress, trying not to wake Kieran. On the floor was a camping cooker and a pot. She would boil water and hope that Kieran had brought tea bags.

Melody slipped on her boots and went outside. It was bitterly cold, but clear and calm. A beautiful crystal-white landscape stretched before her. The shock of the cold air penetrated her head.

He had told her he loved her. So why was her heart not singing, and why was she afraid of him waking up? Was it because she would look into his eyes and see doubt or rejection? It should be so easy — they loved each other. But they hadn't spoken about Sophie or Barradale or the fact that she was going back to Glasgow.

Last night none of that seemed to matter.

'Melody, let me help you with that.'

Kieran was behind her, at the frame of the door, looking out. His hair was stuck on end, his jaw was shadowed with stubble but he was still the best-looking man she had ever seen. Awkwardly she handed over the pot.

He tilted up her chin and smiled softly. 'No regrets?'

At that her heart did start a tiny tune. Everything was going to be all right.

'We'd better get a move on before Elspeth sends for the mainland rescue team again,' Kieran said. He boiled up tea and packed up his large rucksack. Melody swept up the ashes and tidied up as much as possible. The bothy had a charm to it now that it had lacked before, for now it would always be the place they had declared their love for one another.

They drank down the scalding tea and set off. There was a path leading from the bothy that would take them all the way down the valley, Kieran explained. In the bright clear day she could see it under the covering of snow like a ribbon of slightly sunken ground fringed by tufty grass.

He held her hand and whistled and Melody felt stupidly, incredibly happy. All the rest of it, where they would live, how she would manage her career, would be overcome. None of it mattered because they loved each other. It was a feeling like nothing else she'd experienced before. She wanted to shout down the hillside and let the whole valley share her joy and delight. She stole a glance at the object of her emotions. Kieran winked at her. They didn't need words to hold a conversation.

'You'll want to go and visit Skye

almost immediately, I imagine. I'll give you a lift,' Kieran said.

'Thanks. I do want to see her and make certain she's okay. I need a quick shower and breakfast, then we can go.'

'Elspeth's probably got all that in hand. You never did say why Skye and you were up there anyway . . . '

'Skye's idea. She wanted to talk in private.' Melody hesitated over whether to tell him what Skye had confessed, but she reasoned that Kieran was almost family to Skye and was now more than that to her, so she told him what had happened.

'Poor kid,' was his response. 'I can't believe she's carried that secret to herself all these years. No wonder the two of you weren't close.'

'We couldn't be. Skye thought I'd hate her if she told me, so she shied away from me. It's so sad — all those wasted years we could have been having fun together like sisters should.'

'You can make up for it now. You're loving and giving and you've a real chance to get it right this time.'

Melody nodded in agreement. She would put everything into repairing her relationship with Skye.

'It explains John's quiet nature, too,' Kieran went on. 'If Maeve was worried he'd have another stroke, of course she'd mollycoddle him. I'm annoyed at myself for not being more perceptive. I could've helped them more.'

'You've looked after them as well as you would your own parents from what Mum's told me,' Melody said warmly. She knew from Elspeth that Mr and Mrs Matthews were both dead. Perhaps her parents were a substitute for Kieran. They relied on him like a son, but perhaps he needed them too.

'When you move back to Barradale, you'll be able to look in on them often,' Kieran continued blithely.

Melody froze. Did he seriously expect her to move to Barradale, just like that, at the snap of his fingers? What about her career and her house and her friends? They hadn't even discussed it; he just assumed it.

She walked on with him after a small misstep so he wouldn't sense her discomfort. The irony of it was that she had told him that love conquers all! That a person would sacrifice their living place and work to be with the one they love. She could hear her own voice, loud and impassioned, at her dinner table arguing with him. But now she was in that situation herself, it wasn't so straightforward. She needed time to think, to sort out what she would do. No — she had to say something.

'I haven't made up my mind to come back to Barradale,' she said cautiously, slowly.

'You can't expect me to come and live in Glasgow?' Kieran's voice was raised at the end in astonishment that she could even suggest such a thing. 'What about Elspeth and Rona and Aucher? I can't just up sticks.'

'Neither can I,' Melody said heatedly. 'I've got my career and my house.

Besides, I don't know if I want to live on Barradale.'

They stopped dead on the hillside and stared at each other, neither happy at what they saw.

'There it is then. Melody Harper and her hatred of Barradale.' His voice was deep and accented, and his blue eyes flashed.

'It's not that! I've changed, and I don't mind it or dislike it any more. But living here, away from my home . . . ?' She was floundering, desperate to explain, to get across what a huge thing he was asking of her.

He shook his head in disgust and walked on, leaving her to follow miserably in his snowy footprints. At the edge of the woods the snow miraculously melted away. The sheltered valley was damp but colourful.

'Kieran!' Melody called.

He waited for her under the shelter of a giant oak. It was the one that marked the badger sett. It seemed a long time since she'd been afraid of

Catherine ensnaring him.

He loved Melody — or so he said — but his obvious anger made her heart sink and she felt compelled to explain. There had to be a solution that suited them both.

Then a figure was running towards them through the woods, arms flapping and shouting incoherently. It was Elspeth.

'Rona's missing!' she gasped before she sank to her knees in the moist leaves.

13

They pulled her up, supporting her sagging weight until she calmed enough to tell them, 'She's gone! I can't find her!'

'Tell me from the beginning,' Kieran said soothingly.

'Rona was unsettled when the girls went up the hill yesterday. She wanted Melody to play. I'd explained to her not to make a fuss, that Melody would be back later and she was to wave goodbye nicely, and she did, my little love, she did.' Elspeth pressed a trembling hand to her lips.

Melody put her arms around her, trying to comfort her.

'But she became agitated when they were away so long. She overheard me on the phone to Tam and when she saw I was worried she got hysterical. I had to calm her down. I thought she was okay — she and Beezer were watching TV — but she must have seen you go up the hill with Tam and Geoff, and of course you didn't come back either . . . '

'When did you notice she was missing?'

'She was up very early for breakfast at about half past five, but that's normal. She had cereal and a glass of juice as always, then she fed Beezer. That's her special job and she takes it very seriously, she would never leave without doing that. I had my own breakfast at six and was going to suggest a board game to distract her until you two came back, but I couldn't find her.'

'We'll find her,' Kieran assured her, leading the way to the big house, half carrying Elspeth who was so distraught that she could barely walk.

Melody made sure she was sitting at the kitchen table and made her a cup of hot, sweet tea. Kieran was on the phone to Tam and Geoff organising a search party, his voice grim and clipped. Their disagreement was pushed to the side with this new crisis and Melody saw that Kieran was controlled and very much in charge. The men would do his bidding, and gladly. They were all fond of Rona, and Kieran was a fair and generous employer, from what she'd seen and knew about him.

'Have you searched the cottages?' he asked Elspeth.

'Some of them, not all. I looked in Melody's first because I knew you weren't there and wouldn't mind.' Elspeth looked at Melody with a tear-stained face and Melody nodded. 'But I couldn't go into some of the occupied ones. I've got the master key, of course, but some of the couples and families might still be in bed so I didn't feel it right to burst in on them.

'I suppose I thought I'd find her playing in the field or at the edge of the woods. She has a lot of imaginary games and when she's playing them she loses track of time. It's happened before but she's never been away this long.'

Kieran picked up the phone again. 'I don't care if people are asleep, we need to be absolutely certain we've checked all the houses on the estate. I'll get Tam to organise a search of all the other cottages, then we'll do the outhouses and the barns.'

'And there's the old ruined cottage beyond the second field. She's played in that before.' Elspeth rose with renewed energy and hope. 'I'll go there now and check. Why didn't I think of it?'

Kieran pushed her down gently but firmly. 'Elspeth, leave it to me and Tam. It's good you remembered the ruined cottage and we'll search it, but the best thing you can do now for Rona is to be here for when she returns. She's probably off playing and has forgotten and when her tummy's ready for lunch she'll be back. You need to be here when that happens.'

'Yes, yes you're right. I'll make lentil soup. It's her favourite,' Elspeth said, grasping the hope Kieran had given her.

But Melody saw the fear in Kieran's

eyes as he turned to the phone to tell an exhausted Tam what to do. Melody felt terrible; the estate workers were barely returned from rescuing Skye and taking her to hospital. They could hardly have a had a full night's sleep before they were being called out again on another rescue mission. They would do it without complaint though, she was sure. Kieran's strong commanding voice was enough to ensure that, even without their loyalty to Aucher.

'What can I do to help?' she asked.

Kieran looked at her as if he'd forgotten she was there and refocused on her. Their night on the hill seemed to be in a different life altogether.

'You could help Geoff search the woods. Rona's only allowed on the edge of the trees where they meet the field. She's not allowed in the woods themselves but maybe she's strayed in.'

'What are you going to do?' Melody hoped he was going to say he was coming with her. She needed some small token, an acknowledgement from him that last night had happened.

Yes, it should take a back seat to the job of finding Rona, but could he give her a sign of what he felt? He'd been so angry with her on the way down the hill and now it was unfinished business. She wanted to know that they were all right and could work things out, given a chance to do so.

'I'm going to grid-search the out-houses. Aucher's a massive estate with far too many old and disused buildings on it. I've been saying for a couple of years now that I'd like to demolish them. I wish with all my heart that I'd done so!'

Without another look at her, his lips set in a grim line, Kieran strode off, leaving the two women alone in the big house.

* * *

Melody was bone-tired. She tramped through the woods as if her legs were wading in treacle. Her head was fuzzy and stuffed with cotton-wool and her throat was raw from calling for Rona. She could see Geoff ahead, searching a wet thicket of browned bramble, his grizzled head bobbing as he looked up and down. Where was Rona?

Melody's lack of sleep was catching up on her but fear kept her going. Rona was only a small child. She could hide anywhere, and she knew Aucher a lot better than Melody did. She couldn't begin to imagine all the things that could befall a child out here in the wild wood. If Rona was unconscious or lying somewhere injured, how quickly would they find her?

Melody thought of Kieran's set expression as he left the house. He'd realised much quicker than she had all the horrific possibilities. She sent up another prayer for Rona. *Please God, let us find her safe and well.*

She walked on, looking left and right, hoping for a glimpse of colour different to the sombre browns and greys and olives of the trees. Rona was wearing a bright red jersey and blue jeans. A flash of crimson here would stand out like an emergency flare.

There was the old oak tree now, and beyond it the snowline. The peaks were vanilla against a smear of blue in the stunning day but Melody took no delight in it. Too much had happened since she and Skye had set off so cheerfully yesterday.

She wondered how Skye was. She hadn't even had a chance to visit her and hoped Skye would understand.

Beyond and to the right Melody saw the start of the outhouses and Kieran walking out of one. She waved and ran towards him. 'Any luck?'

He shook his head. 'I'm going through them methodically but nothing yet. The guys are working away too. Any news and I'll get it immediately.' He indicated a walkie talkie handset in his belt.

He looked at her closely. 'You look washed out — are you all right?'

'Yes, I'll keep going like you because

242

I have to until Rona's safe.' Her voice cracked a little. She was very fond of Rona too.

Kieran pulled her close and stroked her hair. 'We'll find her.'

She revelled in his comforting embrace, drawing strength from it. He was still hers in this moment.

'I've got to keep going,' Kieran said with a final hug. 'We'll talk later, you and me.'

Melody nodded. He was right. She kissed him fleetingly, a light touch on the lips for reassurance, and they went their separate ways.

★　★　★

The small group sitting around the kitchen table was white-faced and solemn.

'We've looked everywhere,' Kieran said, scratching the back of his head. 'I don't understand it. I've sent the guys out again. We'll redo the outhouses and the woods and fields.'

'I phoned her friend's mother,' Elspeth said bleakly. 'She isn't there but Chrissie'll put the word round the village.'

'Could she have walked to the shops?' Melody asked.

Elspeth shook her head. 'She wouldn't try that. It's miles and she wouldn't know the directions, so I don't think so.'

'We've tried everywhere,' Kieran repeated, thinking hard.

Elspeth shot out of her chair with an ear-splitting scrape of wood on tile. 'No, we haven't!'

Kieran stared at her.

'The pond,' Elspeth whispered, her eyes huge with dread.

'She wouldn't go there. She knows it's out of bounds . . . ' But Kieran's voice trailed off and all three of them were gripped by a terrible certainty. As one, they ran from the big house down the path to the cottage where the pond lay nearby.

Melody hadn't looked at it properly before. It was large and covered in the leaves of water lilies. They floated on dank green, still water. It was ominously silent; there were no birds or fish or insects giving it life.

'She wouldn't come here . . . ' But Kieran's voice lacked conviction. He looked for a moment as if he would break down and cry but pulled his shoulders back, tightened his jaw. 'We need poles and nets and waders.'

Bile rose in Melody's throat at his words. Rona couldn't be in there! Please God, no! She turned Elspeth away from the pond.

'Do what you have to do. I'm taking Elspeth for a rest. She's falling to pieces.'

Kieran's gaze was serious as he looked at Melody. A message passed between them. They were working as a team, working together and it made them stronger and better. She smiled but her lips trembled and she turned with Elspeth towards her borrowed cottage. This way they were near enough if they got news, but far enough away so they didn't need to see the ghastly sight of the pond being dredged.

'It's all my fault,' Elspeth rambled, clutching Melody's hand, 'I knew she was upset. I should never have left her alone.'

'You couldn't know she'd take off,' Melody said. 'You're a great mum, Rona's such a happy child usually and she loves you so much.'

She guided Elspeth in to the cottage and settled her on the sofa. 'I'll make a pot of tea in a moment, but first, if you don't mind, I'm going to change out of these wet trousers.'

All the tramping through the wet woodland had soaked her clothes but she hadn't noticed until she stopped. Now she was chilled and it wouldn't do anyone any good if she couldn't search or support because she got ill. She climbed the narrow staircase feeling the pull of her aching muscles, and sank down onto her bed. She pulled her boots off one after the other with a clunk. It felt good to let her feet breathe and she wiggled her toes.

Out of the high window she could just see the pond and the men stooping round its edges. One of them, Geoff she thought from his cap of grey hair, was wading in. She hoped they found nothing.

A faint rustle pricked at her ears. At first she ignored it; there were mice in these old buildings, Elspeth had confided in her, despairing of ever ridding the properties of them entirely.

There it was again. A definite rustle and squeak, not coming from the attic ceiling but from under her bed. Puzzled, Melody put her head down between her legs and hung low to look under the bed. There was nothing there. She swung up, feeling dizzy as the blood drained from her head too suddenly, and she waited . . . a beat and a half . . . yes, a definite rustle.

She swung under the bed, snaking her body into the tight space. The bedclothes had fallen down the side of the bed between it and the wall, forming a bulge. As she stretched her arm out to it, the bulge rippled. Melody yelped and jerked back, snagging her hair painfully on the mesh on the underside of the bed. The hurt helped. It was no demon, and it was too big to be a mouse.

'Rona?' she called out.

The bedclothes shuffled apart in wrinkled heaps and Rona was there in the middle, like a bug in a cocoon.

'Rona! You're okay!'

'I'm in my den,' Rona said, pulling up the blanket to her as if to hide once more. Then she let it fall and her face split into a happy grin. 'You went up the hill and I thought you weren't coming back, but you're back now!'

'Yes, I'm safe and so's Uncle Kieran. Come out now, Rona, your mummy needs a cuddle.'

Elspeth would need more than a cuddle to get over her experience. Rona crawled out of her cocoon and sidled out from under the bed, dragging a large book with her.

By this time Melody had run to fetch an ecstatic Elspeth and relieved Kieran.

Elspeth hugged Rona fiercely, her face buried in her daughter's curly hair.

'What were you thinking of, hiding away like that, kiddo?' Kieran asked gently, hunkering down to his niece's level.

'I was sad. You went away and didn't come back.'

'I had to rescue Melody and Skye from the big snowstorm, but I always come back. That's my job, looking after you and Mummy — always,' Kieran declared.

Rona nodded, unconvinced. 'I made a den.'

'It's a clever hidey-hole,' Kieran agreed. 'Mummy didn't see you at all when she was looking here.'

'I was quiet like a little mouse.' Rona put a finger to her lips.

'But what were you doing here all that while?' Elspeth asked hoarsely. She had run out of tears, both terrified and happy, and was now left with a raging sore throat.

'I'm going to make dresses, like Melody.' Rona held up the book and Melody saw it was her fabric scrapbook. 'I'm going to live in the city and wear pretty dresses every day.'

A wave of guilt hit Melody like a tsunami. She had told Rona she could visit the cottage and look at the book any time, but Rona could so easily have wandered off via the forbidden pond, lost in her own world of dreams — dreams that took her far away from Barradale and into Melody's world.

She looked at the three of them. Kieran had his arms round Elspeth and Rona protectively as if he would never let them go, and Melody realised he never would. She had let herself imagine a future with Kieran without thinking, really thinking, of the practicalities. He had spoken more than once about family and responsibility and duty, and his duty and responsibility lay here with Elspeth and Rona. He was right when he said he couldn't 'up sticks'. He could never leave.

But Melody didn't belong here. She was too like Sophie. She had almost put Rona in danger with her influence, making the little girl wish for magic in her life with the fabrics and stories of designing and parties and the glittering lights of the city. She had risked Kieran's life too when he had to rescue her from the hill. She was no outdoor enthusiast and she had no experience of surviving up there.

Melody made her decision. It was never going to work between them. Was there even room for her in Kieran's heart after he saw his duties carried out in Elspeth and Rona and Aucher, or was she forever going to be second-best? If she didn't fit in, would he blame her and compare her to Sophie? She couldn't bear that.

She would go back to Glasgow. In time he would forget her. Or failing that, he would come to understand that it was best for both of them.

She tiptoed out of the room unnoticed. Once they'd taken Rona up to the big house for food, she would pack her belongings and she had just enough time to visit Skye before she left. There was a late ferry or, if it was fully booked, there was the tiny airport which she'd flown in to for Fiona's funeral.

Melody was leaden. It didn't matter her mode of transport. Once she was off Barradale, she was never coming back.

14

Preparations for the wedding show were in full production. The gang and their associates had hired a hall in the cheaper end of Glasgow's Merchant City. As Harry put it, 'It sounds swanky and it'll get the punters through the doors. Once they're in they'll be so wowed by your gorgeous dresses, darlings, they won't notice the scabby, hideous rooms.'

He was in charge of disguising the grubbiness of the venue and could be seen hourly running with swathes of colourful drapes to hang on the walls alongside the publicity banners. These were all home-designed and produced, but glorious and eye-catching because they were made by art school graduates.

Harry was nervous around Melody, like a puppy keen to show affection but afraid of being kicked.

'Got what you need, sweetie? If you want a longer slot for your catwalk just let me know. Oh, and I got you the most fabulous model for you to hang your dresses on.'

Melody nodded and smiled at all the right moments, like a dance she knew blindfold, but her heart wasn't here. She should be swooning to have an opportunity to display her designs to a potentially large audience, but all she could think of was Kieran.

He hadn't phoned or made contact in any way since she'd slipped away from Barradale two weeks before. It was the plainest signal she could receive that he didn't care. He had said he loved her in the heat of passion, but in the clarity of the day, he clearly didn't, otherwise he would have called or followed her. They had never finished their argument coming down the hill — and now they never would.

Melody was still unsure what her answer would be to giving up her entire life in Glasgow and moving lock, stock and barrel to Barradale to be with him. However she wanted the chance to discuss it and decide together. But pride wouldn't let her phone him, so she closed up her heart and put on her bravest face — which obviously wasn't working, because everyone was being so nice to her.

Everyone except Catherine, who had a steely glint in her eye and was spending her time snapping orders at Jade as she prepared her collection for display at the show.

'Hey, this is wonderful. What a fantastic idea to use cambric and passementerie on the bodice. It's like a modern take on a seventeenth-century gown,' Sara said enthusiastically.

She laid the wedding dress down again carefully and gazed at Melody.

'What is it? There's something wrong. You're usually so upbeat and energised. Don't take this the wrong way, but you look like you could use a good sleep . . . and your hair . . . I'm your friend so I should be the one to say it, you need to tidy it up and get your glad rags on. Not a pair of dingy jeans and a plain tee. Come on, girl, it's a fashion show after all, and tomorrow is the grand opening!'

'I'm fine, really.' It took an inordinate amount of effort to even find the words. Melody had spent most of the fortnight alone at home preparing her dresses and mulling morbidly over all that had gone wrong. Even Sara's kindly tone threatened to make her burst out crying.

She had to hold it together at least until after the show. Then, Melody promised herself, she would take a holiday. She'd always fancied visiting the Italian Lakes. She would book herself into a quiet hotel for three weeks and hope that she could start to heal. Failing that, she could pamper herself in solitude, lick her wounds and come out ready to face the world. Which she was most decidedly not ready to do right now.

'It's that guy on the island, isn't it?' Sara guessed. 'Jade said there was something going on between you. I must say I didn't believe her — I thought he was quite taken with Catherine — but I was obviously wrong.'

Melody winced. Maybe it was she, not Sara, who was wrong. And yet her instinct still told her that Kieran was to be trusted. He would not have acted so enamoured of Melody while pursuing someone else.

Why hasn't he called you then? Her fickle heart, supposedly empty and shut, gave a painful squeeze.

'There's nothing going on between us,' she said, the words strangling in her throat. She smiled tightly at Sara.

Sara looked hesitant. Then she sat down beside Melody, dropping her pile of promotional boutique leaflets carelessly on the floor.

'Melody, I know we haven't seen eye to eye recently on some occasions.' She paused as if searching for the right words. 'And I'm really sorry. It's like we've drifted apart from being best friends and I hate it. I miss you. The thing is, you've been kind of wrapped up in your own life, what with your work and Skye and then going to Barradale. And, well, I've been having my own problems. Niall and I haven't been getting along and the boutique is in dire straits.'

'I didn't know.' Melody was so ashamed she hadn't noticed. Sara was right, she'd been too caught up in her own life. 'How badly are you struggling? You won't have to sell it, will you? What about Niall? You're still together?'

Sara held up her hands to stem the flow of questions and retied her dark, shiny hair in its scrunchie before she went on.

'It was touch and go for a while with the boutique, in spite of Harry's good work writing articles about us. Then he introduced us to Catherine and she seemed like a godsend. It's not very nice but we did curry favour with her . . . ' She stopped, blushing bright red, both of them remembering the night of Harry's birthday party.

'We needed her clothes and her name and it was working. The only problem was that Niall was a bit too friendly with Catherine so we were arguing all the time. I was jealous, I admit it. Nothing happened between them but she was flirting like mad with him and he was lapping it up. It's all right now — she's backed off, found other willing victims, like poor Harry — and Niall and I are patching things up.

'In fact, I'd say our relationship is actually stronger for it. Catherine doesn't realise she did us a big favour.' Sara gave a snort of ironic laughter. 'We're not taking each other for granted any more. It's like dating again but with the security of love behind it.'

Catherine. She was poison to everyone she touched, Melody thought.

She looked over to where the catwalk was being constructed from sheets of timber. Harry was rushing about getting in the carpenter's way. Catherine was shouting at him, arms folded across her chest. Behind her, Jade, red-faced with effort, was carrying bundles of material in the direction of the stage.

'I'm glad you told me all this,' Melody said. 'And I'm really sorry I didn't notice anything. Although I did feel a distance between us.'

'It's gone now,' Sara told her firmly and gave her a swift, awkward hug. They weren't the hugging kind of friends, but that was okay. It was good to have Sara back on her side.

'So tell me about Kieran,' Sara urged.

'I'm in love with him but he doesn't love me back, so I'm getting to grips with it. I'm going to concentrate on the show and immerse myself in fashion.' Easier said than done.

Sara wisely said nothing more on the subject. 'Well, come on then. I'll introduce you to your model. She's an art student and perfect for this gorgeous creation. I'm hoping like mad that I get to sell this in the boutique after the show?'

The model was, as Sara described, perfect with a shape to die for. Melody immediately pictured her top creation, the seventeenth-century bodice and skirts, hanging beautifully on the girl's slender but curvy frame. Her brain was in work mode, leaving her heartache to simmer, never-ending, in the background. She was emotionally desolate but she could still function mechanically, she decided. She would survive if she could weather the next few days . . . weeks, months . . . years . . . ? How long would it take to get over Kieran Matthews?

* * *

'Need more space?' Harry asked, rushing to a halt beside Melody. His eyes flickered to the murano glass beads on the bodice and the intricate ribbon lacing and a strange expression flitted across his face.

'Are you okay, Harry?'

'Yes, brilliant darling, just brilliant.

Got to run, Jade's ripped a hem and is having a freaky fit.'

'I'm sure she is. Catherine will no doubt tear an equal strip off her if she finds out,' Melody remarked.

Harry's face darkened, then he pasted on a bright, trademark Harry Gordon smile and whirled away.

Melody watched him go. She'd never seen Harry so stressed out before. It wasn't just the show, for Harry was an old hand at organising events. Yes, there was always a peak of adrenaline and a fear that something would go wrong, but he was very good at getting people organised.

People loved Harry, it was as simple as that. He had an endearing, boyish eagerness that caught people up in its wake. It helped, too, that he was irresistible to most women. They fell over themselves to help him out and Melody had seen him use this to full advantage when asking for volunteers to run events and displays. No, there was something more bothering Harry and

Melody was fairly sure what — or rather who — that was.

She left the young model with the rack of dresses and wandered up through the main hall. The stage was ready, tidy and decorated and there were shouts as the backstage crew attempted to sort out the lighting. The catwalk was nearly complete, although there was still a considerable amount of hammering and swearing going on.

She found Catherine's collection in a side room — she had been given a small room all to herself. Melody smiled wryly. No doubt that was Harry's doing. She walked in casually. There was no one there, but the dresses were fanned out on clean cotton sheets for a last long inspection. There were some stunning designs and very clever innovative details . . .

Then Melody saw it, half hidden by a long, silk skirt. She pulled the skirt carefully aside and in front of her lay a bodice almost identical to the one waiting in her own section of the main hall. There were the intricate ribbons and the tiny, glass beads. The shape and style of the cloth were identical to her own design. Melody stared. This was almost exactly like her most recent dress. She had given a copy of the design to Harry, that night at the Barradale Hotel. He was supposed to write an article about it and photograph the sketches, followed by taking the image of the actual dress when it was finished.

Instead he had gone straight to Catherine Sommerlee and handed over Melody's most private, precious work. She felt sick and numb. Harry was her friend. Why would he do such a thing?

All her suspicions about the previous magazine articles and Catherine's other collections came flooding back. Harry must have been betraying her for quite some time. But Catherine had never before been so completely blatant about her theft. There had been a hint here, a trace there, of Melody's creations but nothing she could absolutely claim as downright copying.

Until now.

A slight noise behind her made her spin round. Catherine Sommerlee stood there, a strange little smile playing on her lips and her dark eyes were mocking. She tucked a strand of pale hair behind her ear slowly and deliberately.

Melody brushed past her and walked fast, down the hall to the bathroom where she was horribly, completely sick. She washed her mouth and face with shaking hands and looked at her white face in the mirror.

Sara was right. She needed to get it together. Her hair was wayward, the thick auburn waves twisting wherever they wished and in need of a comb. Her eyes were bruised from lack of sleep and her skin was pallid.

Harry, Harry, Harry. She couldn't leave it any longer; she had to confront him. It would mean the end of their friendship.

What would Kieran advise? The thought popped into her head and she longed for him with a piercing intensity that made her cry aloud. It wasn't a simple, overwhelming attraction to him; it was the man himself with his strong moral code and his certainty of what was the right thing to do. If only he was here to discuss it, to cuddle her and reassure her and to back her up with his love.

She bit down on her lip until it hurt. She'd never felt so completely and utterly alone before.

* * *

Harry was still frenetically on the go when Melody grabbed his arm. He resisted, but she was as tall as him and had a steely determination on her side.

'Hey sweetie, I'm terribly busy . . . ' Harry's voice faded when he saw her expression.

She pulled him, now unprotesting, into an unused small room and shut the door.

'What's this all about?' But his voice lacked conviction.

He knew. His blond hair was trendily spiked and his blue eyes innocent in his boyish face. Was he really hoping to sail through this and come out the other side unscathed?

'Why did you do it?' Melody asked.

'Do what? I don't know what you're — '

'Give it up, Harry!' Melody cried. 'You were my friend, that's the worst part.'

Harry staggered backwards and landed heavily in a fortunately placed chair. He put his head in his hands. Melody waited. When he looked up he had such a look of guilt and terror she wanted to comfort him, to tell him it was okay. But she didn't. Harry had to tell the truth. After a moment, he did.

'It was Catherine. She's . . . well, you know what she looks like. She's the most beautiful woman I've ever seen in my life. And you know my weakness for women, I was smitten by her. She kept promising that we'd be more than friends. She invited me out to dinner and I thought, this is it, she likes me. But over dinner she started talking about you. She'd met you briefly at a workshop and seen some of your stuff. She asked me to show her some of your designs . . . '

'Why did she think you could do that?' Melody asked coldly.

It was one thing knowing what Harry had done; it was another hearing it from his own lips. She felt as if she would never be warm again.

'I'd told her about you and what a great designer you are and I'm afraid I'd rather boasted that I had an exclusive on your new designs. So she knew that she could get a sneak preview of what you were creating through me.'

'You're despicable, Harry Gordon!' Melody declared.

Harry shook his head shamefacedly. 'I shouldn't have done it. It was truly awful of me, I know it, but I was weak. She told me that it was only once, just out of curiosity and I believed her. But then, once she'd seen that set of sketches she demanded more and I said no, Melody, you have to believe me!'

'But you did give her more. I saw the magazines and I've just seen my favourite, finest design on Catherine's floor,' Melody snapped, her eyes aflame.

'Yes, I did.' Harry's face was guiltily downcast. 'She threatened to tell you what I had done. I was trapped . . . '

'She was blackmailing you?' This was more serious than she'd suspected. This was bordering on the realm of criminality.

'I suppose she was, yes . . . ' Harry sounded vaguely surprised, as if he'd just worked it out.

* * *

Catherine was writing notes in a black, leather-bound book when Melody caught up with her. She was cataloguing her dresses, Melody guessed, because it was what she did too before a show. This way, for each numbered creation she could mark how well it showed on the model, any flaws and most importantly, the audience reaction.

269

Not that she had attended many shows. She, like Catherine, was an 'up-and-coming'. In other words, it was all hard slog and self-promotion for varied rewards and the tantalising goal of recognition and regular money coming in.

Which was why it made it all the more puzzling that Catherine would jeopardise all this by stealing another designer's work.

As she stormed out of her confrontation with Harry, Melody had been in no mood to think of a strategy for speaking to Catherine. She was simply bent on venting her anger and wanted to take the woman and shake her and scream at her, just to get it out of her system.

Gradually her pace slowed until she reached the catwalk where she stopped entirely. The carpenter winked, then shrugged when she gazed right through him, not seeing him but visualising a different scenario altogether. She'd once seen Kieran have to deal with a difficult worker, the day they had opened Aucher to the public. The man, an itinerant worker, had made a shoddy job of erecting his end of the marquee. The canvas was sagging and the struts insecure. Kieran had asked him to redo it and the man had argued back.

If it had been Melody she would probably have yelled and argued, most likely putting the man's hackles up. But not Kieran. She couldn't hear what he'd said but she'd heard his tone; deep and calm and measured. The weird thing was, it worked. The man calmed down and between them, he and Kieran had tightened the canvas and secured the supports just before the main crowds arrived.

It was worth a try, she thought. Besides, she wasn't half as angry at Catherine as she was at Harry. Catherine owed her nothing; she didn't even like her. But Harry was her friend and she hadn't screamed at him because in the end, her pity had overtaken her fury.

'Yes, can I help you?' Catherine asked, turning with a sly smile. 'Come to have a look at the competition, have you? Of course I've more in my collection than you have in yours. You've slowed down. Must be all the time you've spent on that hideous island with your family.'

'If you've a big collection it's because you've stolen half the designs. That speeds things up, doesn't it?' Melody said, forgetting her promise to herself not to react.

'Stolen? That's a serious allegation.' Catherine raised a pair of perfectly groomed eyebrows. 'I hope you can prove it?'

She glided across the room to straighten a hem, as if she was done with Melody. Her long sheet of white hair shone like an angel's. Melody clenched her fists and took a long, deep and steadying breath. 'Why did you do it?'

'Do what?' Catherine asked innocently. 'Look, I'm extremely busy here as you can see. I'm serious about this fashion show even if you aren't. If you want a chat later, ask Jade to show you my appointment book. It's filling up fast for next week, so maybe you'd better scurry off and find her now.'

'It's over, Catherine,' Melody said simply. She let her fists relax and dropped her arms to her sides, feeling her hot anger dissipate. Catherine's power over Harry and Melody was gone. She just didn't realise it yet.

The first flicker of uncertainty showed in Catherine's eyes. She fumbled over a button on the dress she was hanging and Melody saw a thread break free and loosen.

'Harry has told me what you did,' Melody said.

'Harry is a liar. Did he tell you that I'd forced him to show me your designs? What rubbish! He's so pathetic that he came drooling to me professing his love and offering me a secret peek at what you were up to. I told him not to be so ridiculous but perhaps some of what I saw filtered into my subconscious. If that's the case, I do apologise.'

'It's you that's lying. Give it up, Catherine, and just tell me why you did it. You're talented in your own right, so why would you need my designs?'

273

Melody gestured at the beautiful clothing scattered around the room. Catherine had organised a rack for her dresses, some were hanging ready while others were spread out waiting for a final inspection.

'What are you going to do about it?' Catherine asked, cutting to the heart of the matter. Her face was paler than normal making her eyes look like dark holes.

'Nothing,' Melody told her, and realised it was true.

She had no wish for revenge now. It was enough that she had stopped it. She had saved poor Harry from continued intimidation by Catherine, and she was no longer dreading to see her ideas already formed under another's name. Looking at Catherine Sommerlee, she felt nothing but repugnance — and a sliver of pity. She was a low creature despite her outward beauty and Melody wouldn't want to be like her in any world.

'I'm going to do absolutely nothing

about it,' she repeated.

Catherine sank into a chair with an expression of relief.

'But,' Melody continued, 'I want you out of our group. I want you to stay away from Harry and I want an answer — why?'

Catherine sat still, the ice queen, regal and controlled again. She nodded and gave a half-smile. 'I've no use for Harry any more anyway, and as for Sara and Niall, they're nobodies. Why did I do it?' She shrugged. 'The truth is, I don't know. Probably just because I could, and it gave me a rush of sorts.'

Melody knew then that she would never get a proper answer out of Catherine because there wasn't one. She was bright and beautiful and talented but somewhere inside her there was a twist, a flaw which brought her unhappiness and discontent — attributes she passed to others with her corrosive touch.

'I'm going to leave you now to get ready for the show. I know you'll do well with your own work but I'm taking this bodice, which is a complete copy of mine.' Melody lifted the material without a protest from Catherine.

She stepped past her, glad the conversation was over.

'There is one last condition,' she said as she was leaving.

Catherine was furious when she heard what Melody wanted, but Melody was absolutely sure she would comply.

15

Kieran had carried Rona back to the big house, expecting that Melody and Elspeth would follow. When he was sure that Rona was all right, he had turned to see only Elspeth in the kitchen. 'Where's Melody? Didn't she follow you up?'

'I think she's still in the cottage,' Elspeth replied. 'Kieran, I . . . I don't feel too good . . . '

Kieran looked at her in concern. It was unlike Elspeth to complain. She was white-faced with beads of sweat clustering on her temples, and as he reached for her, she collapsed. When he felt her forehead, she was burning up with a fever.

He carried her up to her bed and tucked her in.

Then Rona was fractious, asking for her mummy, and it took the combined efforts of Beezer, the television and a family-sized packet of crisps to settle her.

Only then did he discover that Melody had gone.

He stood in her empty cottage, bewildered. Why had she left him? They had an unfinished conversation from their trek down the hill. Then he slammed his hand hard on the wall in frustration. With a sense of anger directed at himself, Kieran recalled his sharp words. He'd accused Melody of still harbouring a hatred of Barradale. She had tried to explain how she felt, but he hadn't let her. He'd stormed on ahead of her like a stroppy teenager.

He walked slowly back up the path to the big house, still thinking hard. She knew he couldn't leave his family and Aucher. It was much easier for her to move from Glasgow. Her career was home-based. Naïvely, he had expected them to work immediately as a couple.

It had seemed so easy — they loved each other. It was swift and sudden but

Kieran knew it was a forever kind of love. He loved Melody in a way that he'd never felt before, even for Sophie, so he had just assumed they would slot together without any fuss — and logically it had to be Melody making the move.

Her protest on the hill had come as a shock, and his view of their future had shifted a little. If she loved him, wouldn't she move without any reserve? Surely she could work anywhere? Maybe he hadn't phrased it well. He picked up the phone to dial her number, then dropped it. The way he felt couldn't be explained over the telephone, or by text or email. He needed to see her in person.

'Kieran . . . ' Elspeth's weak voice called from upstairs.

When he went to see her, she looked dreadful. The hour or two in bed had not improved her; if anything she was worse.

'It's flu, I feel awful,' she croaked. 'Can you please get me some water? And I'm freezing, can I have another blanket?'

He brought her a jug of water and a tumbler, then a hot water bottle and an extra duvet. As he busied himself about these tasks, Kieran realised there was no way he could leave Elspeth and Rona at present. Elspeth was as weak as a kitten, and there was no one apart from him who could care for her and for Rona. As desperate as he was to run after Melody, he could only hope she would wait for him and understand his delay.

* * *

As the days went by, he began to wonder whether Melody really and truly loved him. If she did, wouldn't she have called? Was that why she'd left, because she didn't love him enough? Were her job and her house in Glasgow, surrounded by her friends, more important? If that was the case, he wouldn't follow her. She, like Sophie before her, had deserted him.

But he felt, instinctively, that that was

wrong. She was nothing like Sophie. On the surface, there were similarities — they were both women who liked to dress well, to shop and to admire material goods — but where Sophie had stopped at her own comfort, Melody was a warm, rounded personality, full of kindness to Elspeth and Rona, ready to pitch in and absurdly eager to try new things, like cycling and hillwalking.

She was a trooper, as his mother would have said. There was definitely more to Melody Harper than first met the eye, and he loved her, wholeheartedly.

He was doing the right thing by being here looking after Elspeth and Rona, so why did it feel so wrong? His body and heart yearned to be in Glasgow, but sheer sense of duty kept him here and busy. He fed and played with Rona and he fetched and carried for Elspeth, who was gradually regaining her strength.

Sitting briefly at the kitchen table in a lull where no one demanded anything of him, sipping good, hot coffee, Kieran finally got it . . .

Life was meaningless without Melody in it. Without her he was on automatic pilot, doing the right thing, getting through the day, but half-dead because she wasn't there. And, like a crack letting in the first ray of light, Kieran began to think that he could leave Aucher and move to Glasgow, after all. He would make sure that Elspeth and Rona were well cared for. He wasn't sure how yet, but he knew, absolutely, that he had to be with Melody. He didn't care where.

He rose with a new sense of invigoration and purpose. He would go to Glasgow and see her. He had to believe that she did love him, and he had to ignore any alternatives. Sophie's desertion had left him weak and untrusting when it came to love, but he was ready, with Melody, to trust again.

★　★　★

'Kieran, can we talk?' Elspeth's voice was still weak and scratchy but she was sitting up in bed, her colour was better and the fever was broken.

'Of course, what's the matter?' He sat at the end of the bed. Downstairs he could hear Rona singing to Beezer. Something about a spotty dog and piggley pigs. An occasional bark showed that Beezer was enjoying it.

'I've been thinking . . . about Rona . . . the day she disappeared, it could have ended very differently.' Elspeth shuddered, and an image of the stagnant pond rose up before Kieran, making him swallow convulsively.

'The point is, Rona's growing up,' Elspeth went on. 'She can't be allowed to roam free at Aucher forever. It's time that she and I moved to the mainland so Rona can attend the local school daily, develop her artistic talents, and get to know other kids. There's a wee house on the market, just on the mainland coast, five minutes from where the ferry comes in. Rona could walk to school from it. I want to bid for it.'

She clasped his hand. 'You've looked after us so well and for so long. It's time you thought about yourself and what you want for your future.'

Kieran said nothing for a long moment.

'I would miss you both,' he said finally.

'It's not very far, you could visit so easily and we'd come over at weekends to see you as well — that's if you wanted us to.'

'Of course I'd want you to. I can't imagine Aucher without you. Are you sure about this, Elspeth? Is it really what you want?' he asked earnestly.

'Yes,' she said, coughing. She sat up against the pillows and took a drink of water. 'My only concern is whether you'll manage without me here at Aucher. It's such a huge place to look after. How will you cope with the estate and the house?'

'I've got a good workforce to run the

estate, although the house might be a different matter.' He grinned. If this was what Elspeth wanted, then he wanted to make it easy for her to leave.

'What's happening with you and Melody?' Elspeth asked. 'Why did she leave so suddenly?'

'I don't know, it's complicated. But I love her and I want to make it work. If Melody won't live here then I'll move to be with her. In the end I might even sell Aucher, if that's what it takes to win her back.'

'Go to her,' Elspeth urged him softly.

16

The show had been a massive success. Melody had secured orders and sold her complete collection, so why did she feel so empty? She'd always found dress designing to be fascinating and all-encompassing and it panicked her to feel as if she didn't care what she designed, or even if she ever designed again.

She mooched around in her home, unable to settle to anything. The mannequin stood reproachfully bare in the centre of the living room. She had no new ideas, no half-finished sketches to be eagerly snatched up and added to as inspiration struck her. There was no inspiration to strike.

The phone rang loudly and she picked up.

'Hey, it's Skye here. How are you?'

I'm out of sorts, morbid and

depressed and most definitely listless — take your pick, Melody thought grouchily, but instead she answered, 'I'm fine, how's your ankle?'

Skye had taken to phoning every few days, which Melody was pleased about. It felt as if they were finally getting to be the sisters they always should have been.

'It's still tender but I can walk on it okay as long as I use my crutches. It'll be quite a while before I'm back on my bicycle.'

Melody couldn't help remembering their cycling trip with Kieran. It had been fun and exhilarating and she'd been so surprisingly happy doing such a simple, childish activity.

It was odd, the way images from Barradale kept flashing into her mind. Its windy weather, the seabirds calling, the harsh but picturesque views from the hills and even the smell of the ferry. The images came back with a fondness of memory.

Her time on Barradale recently had

sorted out so many loose ends in her life. She was on good terms with her parents and Skye, in harmony with her whole family for the first time in her adult life, and she treasured it. She swore she would never lose that again — but she couldn't bring herself to visit Barradale just yet. When the pain eased and she could be sure of her emotions regarding Kieran, then she would go. In the meantime, the Harpers were welcome to visit her.

'That's good news. Which reminds me, when are you coming to stay with me?' she asked Skye.

'That's partly why I phoned . . . ' There was a pause on the line, then excitedly, Skye went on. 'I've made a big decision, Melody. Actually, a huge one.'

'Don't keep me in suspense — what is it?'

'I'm applying for college in Glasgow! I want to study business administration. I've got it all planned out. Once I get my qualification I'm going to set up a bed and breakfast in Marne, I'll be my own boss. What do you think?'

'I think it's marvellous,' Melody told her, smiling at her sister's enthusiasm. Skye's low mood was a thing of the past since she'd released her burden of guilt and started coming to terms with her friend's death.

'Will you cope without Mum making your meals and washing your clothes?' Melody teased, half seriously. Skye had a part-time job in a local shop and she had lived at home all her life. It was a huge step to take, moving out and expanding her future.

'I'm ready to move on with my life,' Skye said firmly. 'I'm twenty-six, for goodness sake. A lot of people are married with babies at this age.'

And Melody was thirty, with no one in her life. She wondered whether Kieran still wanted children. Elspeth had told her he wanted a family, but Sophie didn't. She imagined a little boy with black hair and dark blue eyes just like his dad . . .

Stop it! How will your heart ever heal if you keep doing this?

'Melody, are you still there?' Skye's voice from the plastic handset jarred her back to reality.

'Yes, still here. Have you . . . have you seen Kieran and Elspeth at all? How's Rona?'

That's right, Melody, she thought, *plunge the knife into your heart and turn it until it hurts.*

'Elspeth's much better, she's on the mend. I took round one of Mum's casseroles yesterday.'

'What do you mean, she's better? You didn't tell me she was ill.' Skye hadn't mentioned Elspeth or Kieran in her previous phone calls and Melody had been painfully reluctant to ask.

'She had a horrible bout of flu. It started the day you left. I thought you knew, and you didn't seem to want to ask about Barradale so I was waiting until you brought the subject up.'

'Poor Elspeth . . . and Kieran?' There, she'd done it. She'd said his name out loud without crying. Now Skye would tell her he was happily at work on the estate having dismissed Melody easily from his mind.

'Kieran's been wonderful as he always is. Elspeth says she doesn't know what she would've done if he hadn't been there to nurse her and care for Rona.'

Of course. How silly of her. Kieran was stuck on Barradale caring for his family. A tiny flower of hope blossomed in her chest. It was fragile, and the petals were small. But it had rooted. He couldn't come to her because he was tied to his family. But why hadn't he phoned?

' . . . so Elspeth's put in an offer on the house and if it's successful, she and Rona will move at the end of spring.'

Melody had missed the first part of what Skye had said. Elspeth and Rona were leaving the island? What about Kieran? Would he be left all alone at Aucher?

With a jolt that literally made her

heart thud, Melody knew she had to go to him. She didn't care about her dress designing, or her house or her career. She simply wanted him. If that meant living on Barradale — or on the surface of the moon — then so be it. Without Kieran she couldn't settle and couldn't concentrate on anything anyway. Without him she was only half a soul.

'Skye, I'm sorry, I have to go. I've just remembered I need to be somewhere urgently. I'll call you tomorrow. I love you. Give my love to Mum and Dad.'

She dropped the receiver hurriedly as Skye's voice rose in sisterly query at her change of pace. She would take her smaller suitcase, throw in a few essentials and make the late afternoon ferry. But as she grabbed a couple of skirts from the wardrobe upstairs, the door-bell rang.

Impatiently Melody clattered down the stairs. Whoever it was would get short shrift. It was just a sales call and she was in a hurry. She pulled open the front door and stood stock still.

Kieran stood there as if she had conjured him from her dreams. Melody's heart gave a flip and the flower of hope inside her unfurled its petals fully.

'Hello, Melody,' he said, his dark blue eyes questioning.

Her first instinct was to throw herself into his arms and feel the strength of him against her, but she didn't know what he had come to say. She stepped back, aware once more of his height and the breadth of his shoulders as he followed her in. She caught the scent of his aftershave and her nerves tingled. He always had such a powerful physical effect on her. She tilted her chin so she met his gaze, and was blown away by the love and yearning she saw there.

With a gasp of delicious shock, she reached for him and Kieran reached for her too in a kiss that echoed with love and loss and raw desire. The kiss was followed by another, equally needy and passionate and claiming, until Kieran finally drew back from her reluctantly.

He frowned at her suitcase which lay

abandoned on the hall floor. 'You're going away?' There was pain in his voice.

Did he think she was fleeing even further away from him and from Barradale?

'I was coming to find you,' Melody said, kissing him again and running her fingers through his thick, dark hair the way she'd dreamed of so often these last two weeks.

'You were going to travel to Barradale to find me?' Kieran sounded amazed, joyful and incredulous in equal parts.

Melody's chest burst into a kaleidoscope of happiness. He was here, with her. She laughed out loud. 'It's not the ends of the earth, you know!'

'It seems that way though, sometimes,' Kieran said. He put his hands on either side of her face so gently as if she were a rare and precious creation and looked deep into her eyes. 'I love you, Melody Harper. I should've told you more when we were on the hillside. I don't care where we live or what we do as long as we're together.'

'I love you too, completely and utterly and forever,' she told him, her heart singing.

★ ★ ★

'What you said, about me still hating Barradale,' Melody said, a little later when they had calmed enough to sit together in her living room. 'It's not true.'

'I'm sorry, I shouldn't have said it. I know your opinion of the island has changed greatly. It was my fault for assuming you'd move to be with me. We should've discussed it as a couple.'

As a couple. The phrase had such a lovely ring to it, Melody thought happily.

'I just felt that history was repeating itself,' Kieran went on. 'Sophie hurt me more than I knew. I had sealed off my heart so I wouldn't fall in love again, but you burned your way in. When you wouldn't contemplate moving from

295

Glasgow, it brought a lot of bad memories flooding back.'

Melody stood up and went to stare out the window. The outside world was still there, cars moving along the narrow street, the pedestrians streaming past, all oblivious to the little world within her house.

She turned to him soberly. 'I'm nothing like Sophie, you need to know and believe that. I'm never going to leave you, Kieran.'

'I realise that now, but when you left, I thought you didn't love me enough . . .'

Melody sat again with him. There was so much to be said and yet they didn't need words. Their bodies and minds were together, two halves completed.

'When you didn't follow me or phone me, I thought you didn't love me either,' she said. 'I didn't know about Elspeth's illness until today when Skye phoned. That was the trigger — I'd been so foolish waiting for you to make the first move, when I should have been packing to go and find you.'

'I couldn't leave when Elspeth and Rona needed me so much. I was going to phone, but what I feel for you couldn't be said over the phone; I needed to see you in person. So I had to wait and do the right thing, even when it felt so wrong. I wanted to fly to you, my darling, my dearest Melody.' His arm was round her, his fingers stroking the nape of her neck, making the tiny hairs prickle. She wanted more, much more — but there were things she still wanted to know.

'Where will we live? I can make my dresses anywhere.'

'I've been thinking about selling Aucher, actually. I'm fond of it but it's too big for me to run it on my own.'

'But you love the place — you can't sell it!'

'Elspeth ran the cottages for guests. There's no way I can do that and run the rest of the estate and the cycling business too. We'd rattle around in the big house, it's too large.'

'Not if we have a family,' Melody said, unthinkingly.

Kieran looked at her in surprise. 'I didn't know you wanted children. I assumed they weren't in your picture of the future. You're a career girl at heart.'

'I think I'd like some. One or two, at any rate. Not yet, of course, but in a few years' time, yes. Wouldn't you?'

He pulled her to him. 'Yes, very much. I never imagined . . . I'd put it out of my mind to be honest. But yes, a boy and a girl.'

'Or two of each? To help fill the big house!' Melody joked.

'Or a passel?' Kieran grinned. 'I've no idea how many a passel is, but it sounds a lot.'

'As for the holiday cottages,' Melody said, brightening as an idea came to her, 'I might just have the solution.'

She told him of her conversation with Skye and her sister's plan to go to college.

'If you could wait a year until she gets her college diploma, you could offer her the job running the cottages as a bed and breakfast business. I can't answer for her but I'm pretty sure she'd jump at the chance.'

'It would work well,' he mused, then he turned his blue gaze on her. 'What about you? Could your business be run successfully from Aucher?'

'I'm not sure,' Melody admitted. 'But I'm willing to give it a try. It's not a huge commute to Glasgow by ferry or plane for shows and meetings anyway, and I know I can produce the designs and create the dresses at home. It's a bit more tricky for client fittings but it can be done, though it's a matter of being super-organised. That's the hard part — I'm usually a bit scatterbrained when it comes to that side of the business.'

'Would it help if you had an assistant on the mainland?'

'Gosh, yes. It'd make life a lot easier, but I can't imagine anyone wanting the job. It wouldn't pay well, at least initially, as I'm still making my name and it would be part time at most. Who did you have in mind?'

'Elspeth needs something to occupy her while Rona's at school,' Kieran explained. 'And it's not about the money, I take care of that, but I'm certain she'd like to be occupied with something interesting.'

'I'd love that,' Melody said warmly. 'It'd be great working with Elspeth, we get along so well.'

She got up, intending to refresh the coffee pot, but Kieran pulled her down again. She looked at him in surprise. He gave a little cough as if he was about to give a speech and she giggled, but stopped at his serious expression.

'There's just one last thing I have to say to you, Melody.'

'What's that?'

'Will you do me the honour of becoming my wife?'

17

Melody arrived at her parents' house in Marne with a stomach full of butter-flies. Today she was getting married to the most gorgeous man in the world and nervous excitement had been her constant companion for the last twenty-four hours.

She stood in the front garden, savour-ing her last few minutes alone before the hectic flurry of preparation began. The sea was a bright aquamarine, reflect-ing the hot summer sunshine in coruscating twinkles. Her mother's hydrangea was in full blossom of huge old-fashioned blousy pink flowers. The plantains were flowering too, less obviously, with dusty yellow crowns around a black centre.

Melody smiled at them, secretly pleased they'd survived her mother's weeding. Even the birds sounded excited, singing noisily and tunefully from the shrubs.

'Ah, here she is, the bride.' John Harper came out to hug his elder daughter.

'Bring her in then,' Maeve chided him with a wide smile. 'It's the big day, we need to start getting ready. We'll start with a pot of tea to calm the nerves.'

Melody stepped in to the freshly decorated house and thought anew how different the place was. The hallway was all light cream and golden wood flooring, making it light and airy and modern. The living room had lost its ugly picture of the sailing boats and the ancient flying ducks. Now there was a new mulberry three-piece suite, velvet print wallpaper and an attractive brass standard lamp, making the room at once fashionable, inviting and cosy.

'Wow, you finally finished decorating,' Melody commented, putting down her luggage gratefully and stretching her shoulder muscles. Her mother was quick to extract the large box containing her wedding dress so that it could be hung and the creases in the fabric released.

'Yes, we're quite pleased with it,'

Maeve said. 'I hope you don't mind, love, but we cleared your room out completely. We've turned it into a study for your dad. We knew you wouldn't need it now you'll be living in your own home at Aucher.'

Curious, Melody climbed up the staircase to see. All the dusty clutter had gone. It would always be a small attic room but without the bed and the wardrobe, there was sufficient space for a computer desk, chair and bookshelf. She could imagine her dad in here, reading his paper or completing one of his beloved crosswords.

'I haven't thrown out your belongings,' Maeve shouted up. 'They're in the garage, so you can collect them when you come back from your honeymoon.'

Honeymoon!

She was getting married today. It hit her hard and stirred up the butterflies. It was good to be back in Barradale for good, though. She and Kieran had spent too much of the last six months moving between Glasgow and Aucher for work, often spending time apart when they had to. Finally after today, they'd be together forever.

She went back downstairs to the kitchen to find her mother.

'What made you decide to renovate the house?' she asked, not wanting to add that it had remained in a depressing timewarp for the previous thirty-odd years.

Maeve crinkled her eyes and looked at her tall daughter. 'It was just time for a new start. Skye was so happy, she seemed to have shed her ghosts, and your dad and I were so relieved. It lifted a great pressure of worry from us that I don't think we were even fully aware was there. One morning, shortly after Skye left to stay with Kimmy in Glasgow, we both agreed it was time for a change.'

Skye's application to college had been successful, and while the course didn't start until autumn, she was sharing a flat in Glasgow with a friend and enjoying her new independence.

'It's really lovely. You've done a great job,' Melody said, hugging her mother.

'We're taking a proper holiday, too.'

'But you and Dad never travel! It's a cottage up north, is it?'

'No, it's North America. We fly out soon after your wedding.'

'America!'

Her parents had never travelled further than England before.

'I've always had a wee notion to see the Grand Canyon. We couldn't go far away before because we had Skye to consider, but now she's got her own life to lead, well, we've decided to live ours a little, too.

'Come along, Melody love, you need to get that beautiful dress on. We don't want to keep Kieran waiting, do we?'

Dumbfounded, Melody let her mother lead her to where her wedding dress hung on a hanger over the door.

* * *

Melody was left with her spinning thoughts and her favourite dress. Carefully she lifted it down, feeling the satisfying weight of the long, full, silk skirt and hearing the tinkle of the tiny glass beads on the bodice. She hadn't been able to part with this dress at the fashion show. Despite many requests from girls eager to purchase it, she had decided it was not for sale.

She might produce copies of it to sell in the future, but for now she would be the first to wear it. She slid into it and looked at herself in the long mirror thoughtfully provided by Maeve. She saw a woman with flushed cheeks and sparkling hazel eyes, her slim waist accentuated by the bodice. She was curvy, yes, and she'd had to adjust the dress to fit her rather than the model, but today she felt her curves were all in the right place for once.

'You'll do,' she told her reflection.

'You'll more than do,' Skye said behind her. 'You're gorgeous, big sister.'

'Hey, you made it!' Melody shrieked and hugged her.

'Of course. I wouldn't be late for my own sister's wedding.'

Skye was looking great too, Melody thought. The six months away from home had suited her. She was wearing her fair hair longer and her make-up brought out the colour of her eyes and the fullness of her lips.

She'd changed her clothes style, too. Gone were the old jeans and fleeces that she slung on daily without any care. In their place was a trendy black leather jacket over a flowery summer dress. The rock-chick style suited her.

'So where's my bridesmaid dress?' Skye asked excitedly. 'I've brought eyeshadow to match with the burnished copper silk. I still can't believe it took three fittings to get the dress right. Did you pick up my heels for me?'

'No,' Melody said, her eyes widening. 'Skye! You were meant to get them dyed and delivered yourself.'

'Only joking!' Skye laughed wickedly, waving a pair of high heeled copper-coloured shoes at her. Melody pinged her garter at her. It hit Skye on the cheek and she screamed.

The door flung open and Maeve stood there, arms folded and expression stern — even if her eyes were twinkling. 'Girls, quiet down. We're running out of time. Jade's here with the carriage.'

That piece of news had them screaming again and rushing to the window to look out.

Over the low stone wall of the front garden they saw a gleaming open carriage pulled by two chestnut horses in gleaming good health. Jade stood at their heads, holding the harnesses and talking softly to the horses. She was stroking their velvet muzzles and calming them.

'You're not quite ready so I'll invite her in for a cup of tea,' Maeve said, bustling about, every inch the mother of the bride. 'She can tie the horses to the gate.'

Jade came in to say hello once she'd been plied with tea and biscuits. A slight, not unpleasant, aroma of horses travelled in with her.

'Melody, you make a lovely bride,'

she said. 'I recognise that dress — it really suits you.'

Their eyes met knowingly. This was the dress that sparked Melody's showdown with Catherine Sommerlee.

Much as Melody didn't want to think of her on her wedding day, she couldn't help asking, 'Do you know what happened to Catherine?'

Jade nodded. She tucked a curl of red hair behind her ear and Melody noticed that her nails were unbitten, short and neat. She'd lost a little of her extra weight, too. Mucking out the horses and riding were both very active tasks, and Jade was getting fit and trimmer carrying out her work.

'I heard that she's gone off to London. She could hardly stay in Glasgow once word got out about what she'd done.'

'I honestly never said a word,' Melody said, mystified. 'It was very much between her and me. I didn't want her to suffer over all the unpleasantness. I just wanted it to stop. How did it all leak out?'

'Harry, I think,' Jade said. 'You know what a gossip he is, he can't keep a secret to save himself.'

'But wouldn't it reflect badly on him?'

Jade shrugged. 'You know Harry, he bounces back. Everyone loves him. I haven't heard a single bad word about him.'

'Well, at least it's all over,' Melody said firmly.

'I didn't get a chance to thank you properly,' Jade said, smiling a little shyly at her. 'I couldn't understand it, that day at the show, why Catherine was letting me go with a month's extra salary. It was a shock, but also the best feeling in the world to be free of her.'

'But you got the letter, right?' Melody said quickly. Freeing Jade had been her final demand to Catherine. She'd known that the Barradale Stables were looking for new staff and it was an opportunity for Jade to realise her ambition.

'Yes, the offer of a job at the Barradale Stables arrived the day after.

It was like a fabulous dream come true. So, thank you a million times. I'm living my dream and loving it.'

'Talking of which,' Melody glanced at her watch, 'If I don't get my hair done soon I won't make my own wedding — even if the horses gallop.'

'I'll send Maeve in. I'll just check on the horses and get everything ready for your bridal journey to Aucher.'

★   ★   ★

Melody felt the comforting reassurance of her father's arm in hers as she looked along the petal-strewn path which was the makeshift aisle. On either side of it, the wedding guests sat chattering and settling themselves, a rainbow-coloured audience with many pretty hats and fascinators on display.

She couldn't make out individual faces, it was all a blur. All she could see was Kieran, tall and handsome in a dove-grey morning suit and salmon pink waistcoat, grinning at her nervously from under the bower at the end of the path.

They were getting married in the gardens at Aucher on a gloriously hot and sunny day. There were white marquees set up ready with tables and chairs for the wedding meal, and every guest had been welcomed with a flute of champagne by the hired waiting staff.

The wedding march started up and Melody and her father started down the grassy aisle towards Kieran. Rona and Skye, the bridesmaids, followed them. Rona took her job of arranging the bride's train very seriously. Melody's skirt was impeccable under the little girl's keen gaze.

And then she was there beside him and he was squeezing her fingers gently for courage. The minister was speaking and just as her nerves calmed, Kieran was lifting back her veil and kissing her tenderly with all his love.

Her husband. She was now Mrs Melody Matthews. It had a fine ring to it. The crowd of friends and family were applauding and the newly married couple sat to sign the register, the shiny new gold of their matching rings brilliant in the sunlight.

'I love you, Mrs Matthews,' Kieran whispered to her as they clasped hands and went to join their guests.

'I love you too, my darling husband,' she whispered back.

Then her dad was there with two glasses of champagne for the happy couple, and the party took off.

* * *

After a while of mingling with the crowd, she lost him. They had a little while until the dinner, and at some point they would get far too many photographs taken by Harry.

'Congratulations on a super wedding.' Sara caught up with Melody, looking happy and excited.

'I'm glad you're enjoying it. It's good to see you, Sara. We haven't had much time to catch up with each other these past few months. It's been hectic. We must get together once Kieran and I get back from our honeymoon.'

'Do you know where you're going yet?'

'I haven't a clue. It's a surprise, Kieran's organised the whole thing. I don't care where we go, as long as we're together.'

'That's very romantic.' Sara sighed wistfully.

'So, have you been busy? How's the boutique?'

'It's taken off all of a sudden. I was really worried when Catherine left that we'd lose a lot of business without her clothes but happily that didn't happen. It's funny, but girls looking for a wedding dress, once they'd worked with her for fittings and so on, weren't so keen to recommend her to others.

'You're still very much in demand, you'll be glad to know. Your idea of short island breaks combined with dress fittings and design consultations is going a bomb. It's unusual and I'm getting a lot of brides-to-be enquiring about it.'

'That's great news. Of course, I can still do things from Glasgow too, if that's easier for clients. I'm keeping my house on there for the time being as a work base.'

'How does it feel to be a married woman?' Sara asked. 'Any regrets about giving up your freedom?'

'None at all,' Melody answered without hesitation. 'When you love someone as intensely as I love Kieran, it's just perfect. I still have my freedom but now I've someone to share it with.'

At that moment, Sara lifted her hand to smooth her hair, and a sparkle of pure diamond shot out from her finger.

'Now I know why you're asking — you're engaged!' Melody shrieked. 'You didn't tell me.'

Sara looked sheepish and smug and proud all at once. She showed Melody the flawless diamond set in an antique gold ring.

'Niall proposed to me yesterday. It was out of the blue. I said yes immediately before he could change his mind!'

'Congratulations to you both,' Melody said, happy for her friend, who deserved a happy ending after the stress of nearly losing the boutique and the problems between herself and Niall.

'Have you seen Harry yet?' Sara asked.

'No, I've not had a chance to meet up with him for months. To be honest, after the show we were avoiding each other. It almost wrecked our friendship,' Melody went on. 'It could have ended it but I've been friends with Harry for so long, eventually we made up, but I've been busy and Harry's not been around.'

'Want to know the reason he's been so quiet lately?' Sara said with a sly grin.

'He's okay, isn't he?' Melody said, eyes wide with concern.

'He's more than okay. Harry Gordon

has finally succumbed to falling in love!'

'Never!' Melody said, amazed. Harry had been a dreadful flirt and in all the years she'd known him, he'd never shown any interest in any one woman for more than a month or so. 'Who is it? Do we know her?'

'You can meet her yourself,' Sara said in wicked delight. 'Here they come now.'

Melody looked across to the marquee where Sara pointed. Sure enough, Harry was walking in their direction, his arm round a willowy girl who looked vaguely familiar. As they got closer, Melody recognised the girl and smiled. Harry was a sneaky devil! It was the pretty waitress from the coffee shop.

'Mrs Matthews, you make a glowing, blushing bride.' Harry bowed playfully. It was good to see he hadn't changed too much. 'Can I introduce my girlfriend, May?'

'Hello.' Melody shook her hand and Harry's girlfriend smiled back in a friendly manner. 'I think we've met before. You work at the coffee shop in Merchant City, don't you?'

'That's right.' May laughed. 'You have a good memory. Harry is a regular.'

'I became a regular when I saw you,' Harry said with a grin. 'I had to drive each day to get my coffee when I could've got it two minutes up the road from my flat.'

They all laughed. Melody noticed that May was quick to remove Harry's glass. It was done discreetly, but she was glad that Harry had found someone special who cared about him.

'I've brought my camera so just shout when you want the wedding photos done,' Harry said.

'After the meal? I think they're calling us in now. Poor Kieran's dreading giving his speech.'

They walked back to the marquee together, joined by Niall on the way. He put his arm proprietarily around Sara. They were a good gang of friends,

Melody decided. They had come through together and it was good to know they were on her side.

'Melody, there you are,' Elspeth panted. She clutched her wedding hat so it didn't fall off. 'Have you seen Rona?'

'No.' Melody stopped, letting the others go on to find their tables. 'Should we search?' Memories of that dark day and the dredge of the pond flickered at the edges of her mind.

'No, no, it's nothing like that,' Elspeth said soothingly, putting her at ease again. 'Rona's matured a lot these past months. That school's a marvel and she's blossomed there. No, she's going to say a poem for you after the meal, so she needs to come and sit in her place pronto.'

'She's going to read out loud to everyone?' Melody was impressed. 'She can give Kieran a tip or two for his speech!'

Rona came running up, holding her hems high. Beezer trotted slowly after, yellow and pink flowers tucked into his collar.

'Beezer's a flower dog, look!'

'That's great, now straighten your dress. You need to go and sit next to Uncle Kieran and help him with his words.'

Rona nodded seriously and flew off to the marquee. Beezer followed hopefully.

★ ★ ★

The meal was a success, the speeches amusing and the dancing suitably wild for a traditional ceilidh. Kieran caught up with Melody in the cooling evening air where she stood looking out across the Aucher lands.

'I'm going to enjoy making Aucher our family home,' she said softly, turning into her husband's embrace.

'It'll be fun developing it together,' Kieran agreed. 'But first we need to get ready for our honeymoon.'

'Where are we going? Can you tell

me now? I can't take the secrecy any longer,' Melody begged.

'Very well. You'll have to know in any case so you can pack a selection of your flimsiest dresses and highest, most unsuitable sandals,' Kieran teased, trailing a hot blaze of kisses from her neck up to her earlobe and across to her mouth.

She was momentarily distracted while she kissed him back with a rising passion that shook them both. Kieran looked as if he wanted to sweep her off her feet right there and then, away from the reception and into the waiting carriage where they could be alone in the dusk on the way to the airport.

Which reminded her, he hadn't told her yet where they were going. All she knew was that it was a late flight out. Although she didn't want to miss the end of the wedding reception, it was traditional for the bride and groom to be waved off, and she'd seen Jade and Harry tie tin cans and ribbons and balloons onto the back of the carriage earlier. She couldn't disappoint them.

'So?' she prompted, encouraging him by moulding her body to his. She could feel his body heat as he held her close and dropped tiny kisses onto her hair.

'Mrs Matthews,' Kieran murmured, 'How would you like to visit the romantic Italian Lakes?'

'You're kidding!' Melody squealed delightedly. 'However did you know?'

'Know what? I just picked a place I've always wanted to go and visit and I'd love to share it with you.'

'It's my dream honeymoon and my idea of the most romantic place on earth! You really are my perfect man.' Melody kissed him again. 'I love you so much.'

They stood arm in arm, gazing out at the pale green of the fields, the darker verdant of the woodlands in the distance and further beyond, the rim of blue sea.

'And after our honeymoon, we'll return home — to Barradale,' Melody said contentedly.